THIS BOOK BELONGS TO

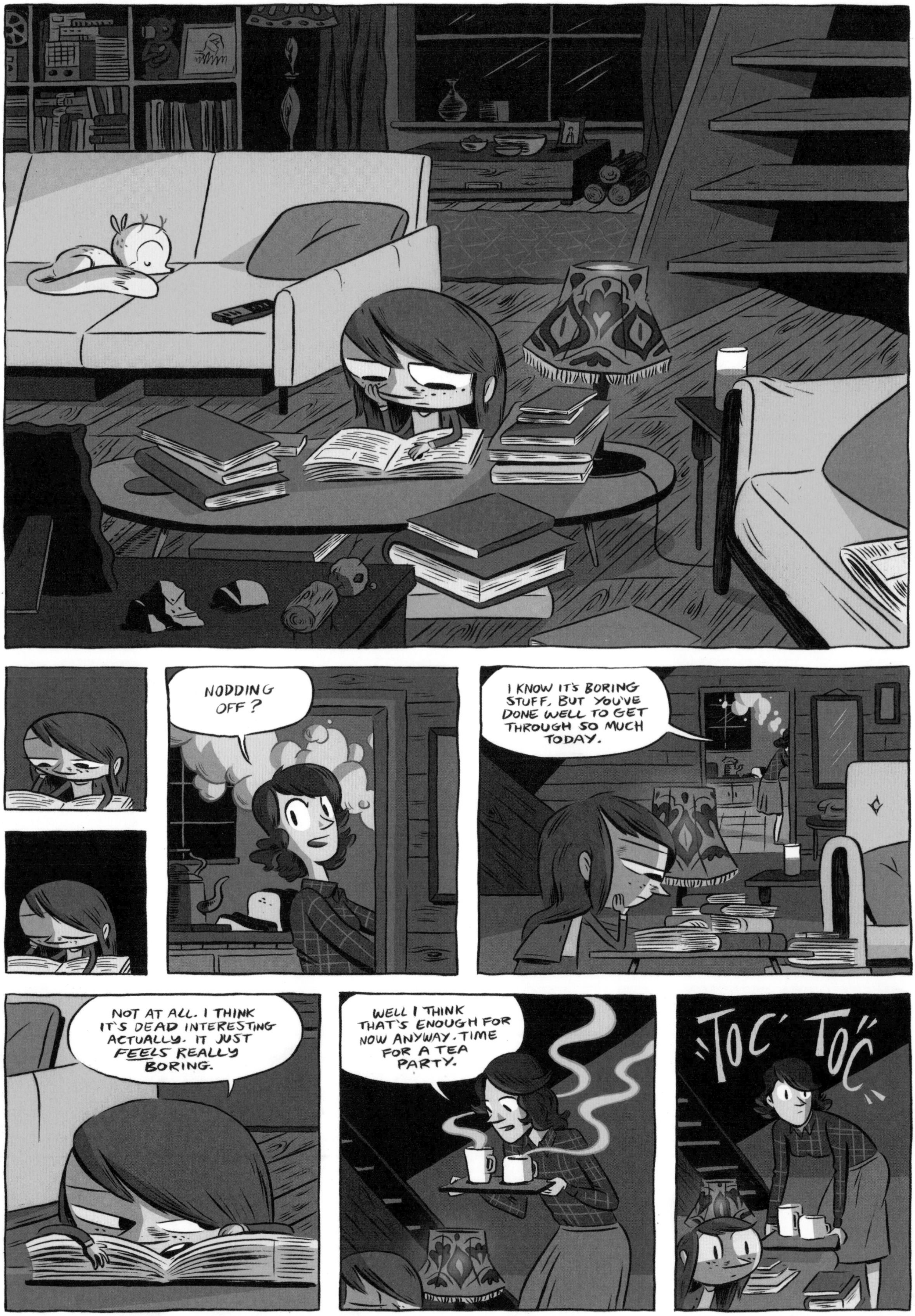
NODDING OFF?
I KNOW IT'S BORING STUFF, BUT YOU'VE DONE WELL TO GET THROUGH SO MUCH TODAY.
NOT AT ALL. I THINK IT'S DEAD INTERESTING ACTUALLY. IT JUST FEELS REALLY BORING.
WELL I THINK THAT'S ENOUGH FOR NOW ANYWAY. TIME FOR A TEA PARTY.
TOC TOC

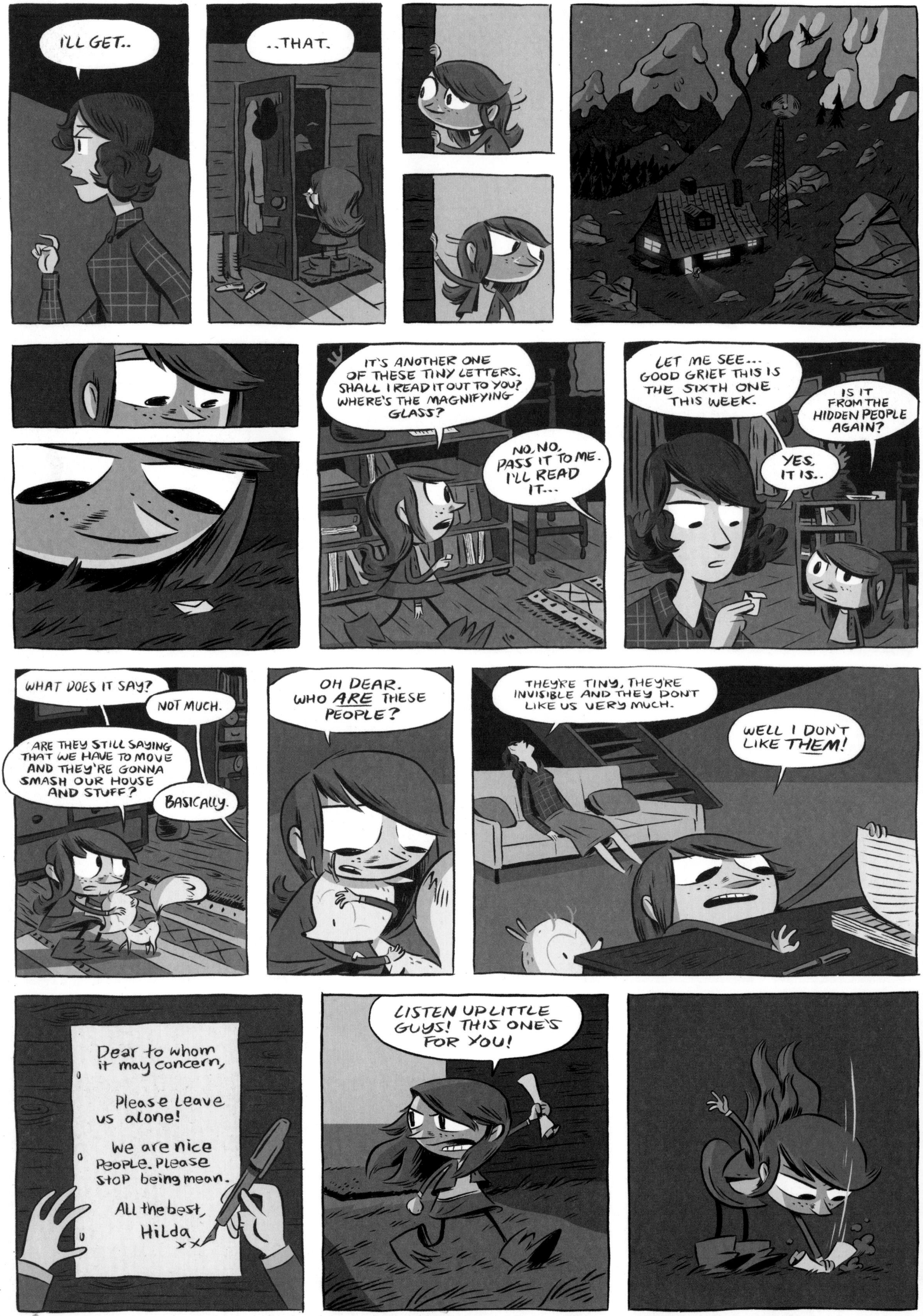
I'LL GET..
..THAT.
IT'S ANOTHER ONE OF THESE TINY LETTERS. SHALL I READ IT OUT TO YOU? WHERE'S THE MAGNIFYING GLASS?
NO, NO, PASS IT TO ME. I'LL READ IT...
LET ME SEE... GOOD GRIEF THIS IS THE SIXTH ONE THIS WEEK.
IS IT FROM THE HIDDEN PEOPLE AGAIN?
YES. IT IS..
WHAT DOES IT SAY?
NOT MUCH.
ARE THEY STILL SAYING THAT WE HAVE TO MOVE AND THEY'RE GONNA SMASH OUR HOUSE AND STUFF?
BASICALLY.
OH DEAR. WHO ARE THESE PEOPLE?
THEY'RE TINY, THEY'RE INVISIBLE AND THEY DON'T LIKE US VERY MUCH.
WELL I DON'T LIKE THEM!
Dear to whom it may concern,
Please Leave us alone!
We are nice People. Please stop being mean.
All the best, Hilda xx
LISTEN UP LITTLE GUYS! THIS ONE'S FOR YOU!

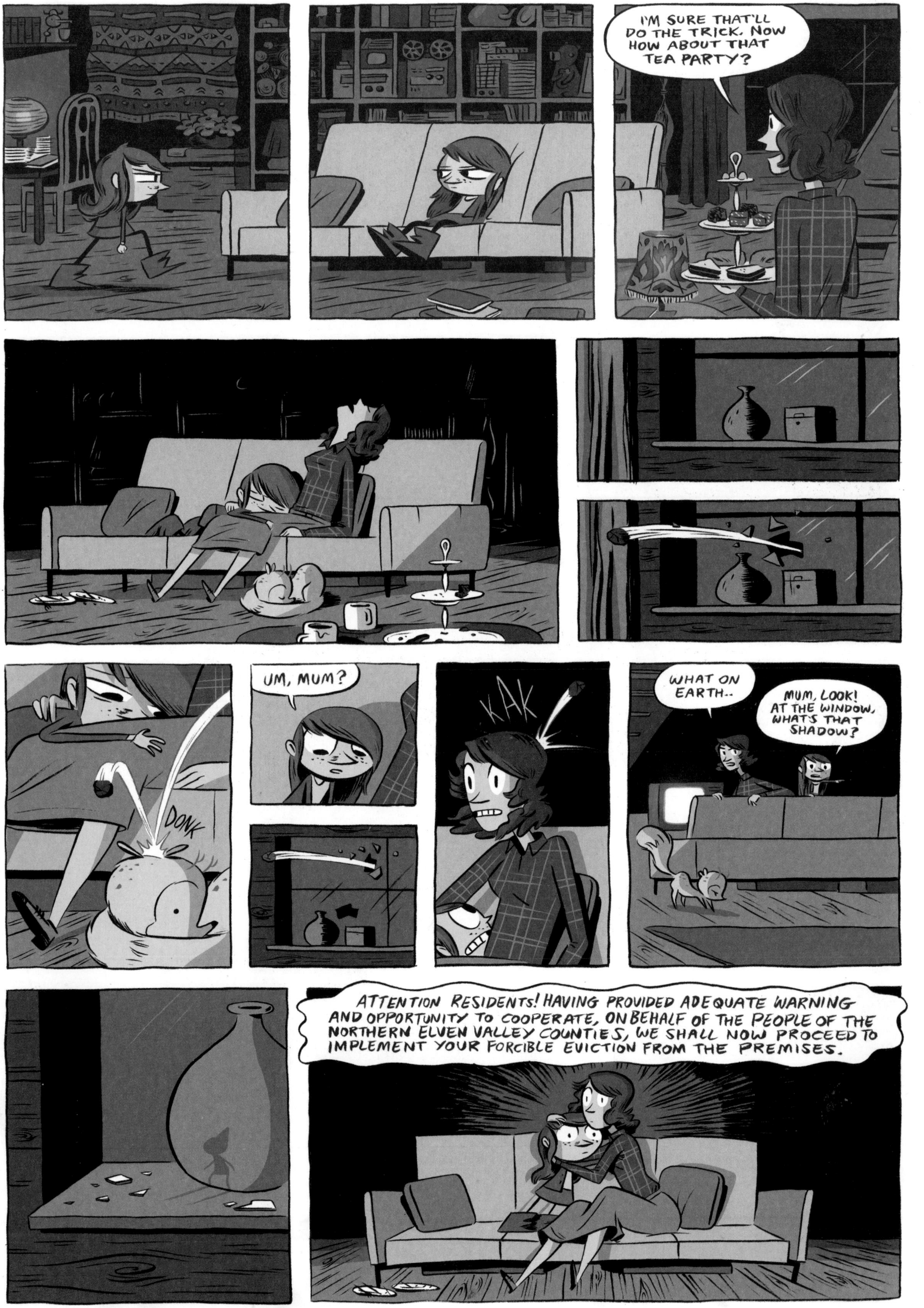

I'M SURE THAT'LL DO THE TRICK. NOW HOW ABOUT THAT TEA PARTY?
DONK
UM, MUM?
KAK
WHAT ON EARTH..
MUM, LOOK! AT THE WINDOW, WHAT'S THAT SHADOW?
ATTENTION RESIDENTS! HAVING PROVIDED ADEQUATE WARNING AND OPPORTUNITY TO COOPERATE, ON BEHALF OF THE PEOPLE OF THE NORTHERN ELVEN VALLEY COUNTIES, WE SHALL NOW PROCEED TO IMPLEMENT YOUR FORCIBLE EVICTION FROM THE PREMISES.

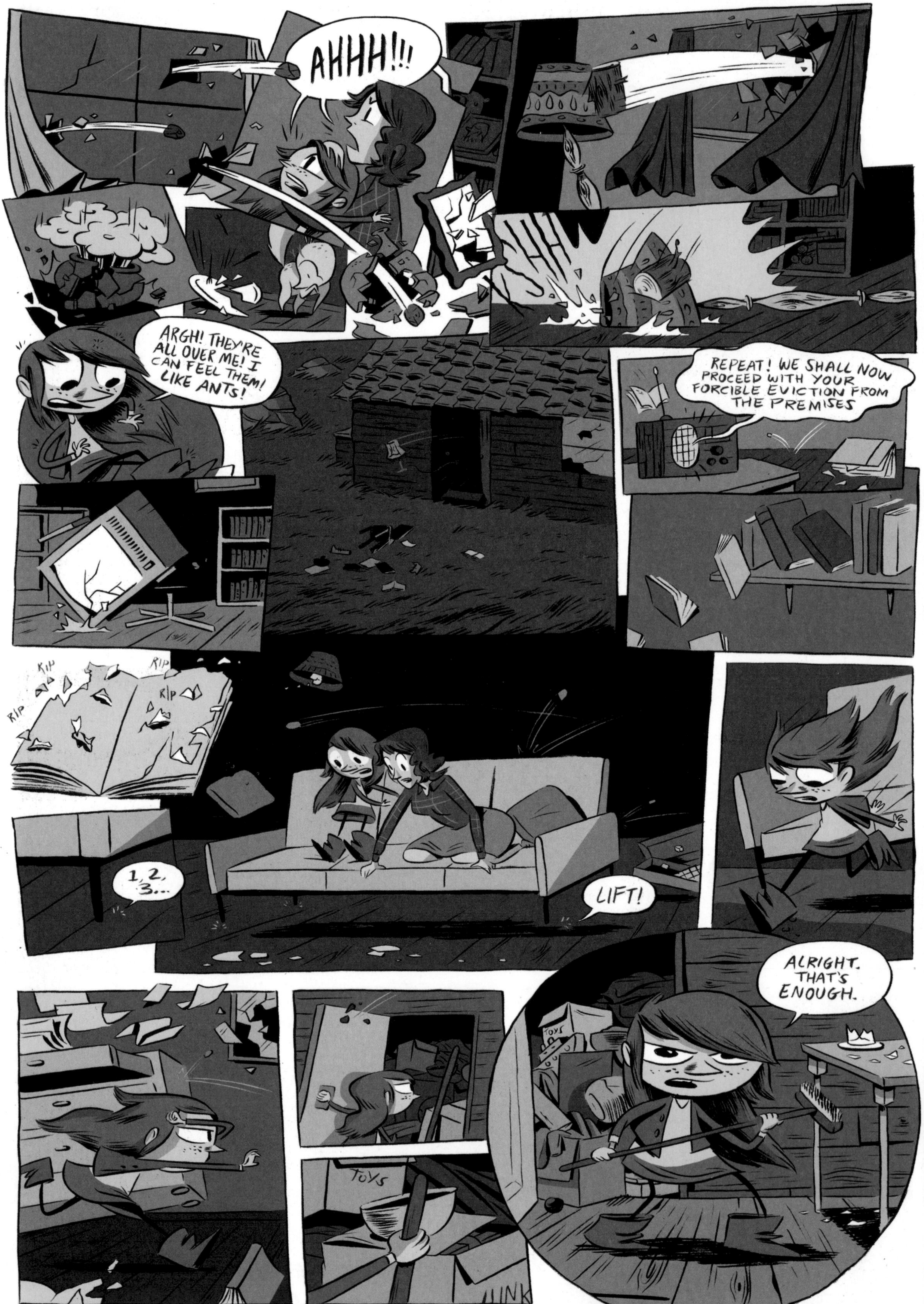
AHHH!!!
ARGH! THEY'RE ALL OVER ME! I CAN FEEL THEM! LIKE ANTS!
REPEAT! WE SHALL NOW PROCEED WITH YOUR FORCIBLE EVICTION FROM THE PREMISES
RIP
RIP
RIP
RIP
1, 2, 3...
LIFT!
TOYS
TOYS
ALRIGHT. THAT'S ENOUGH.
LINK

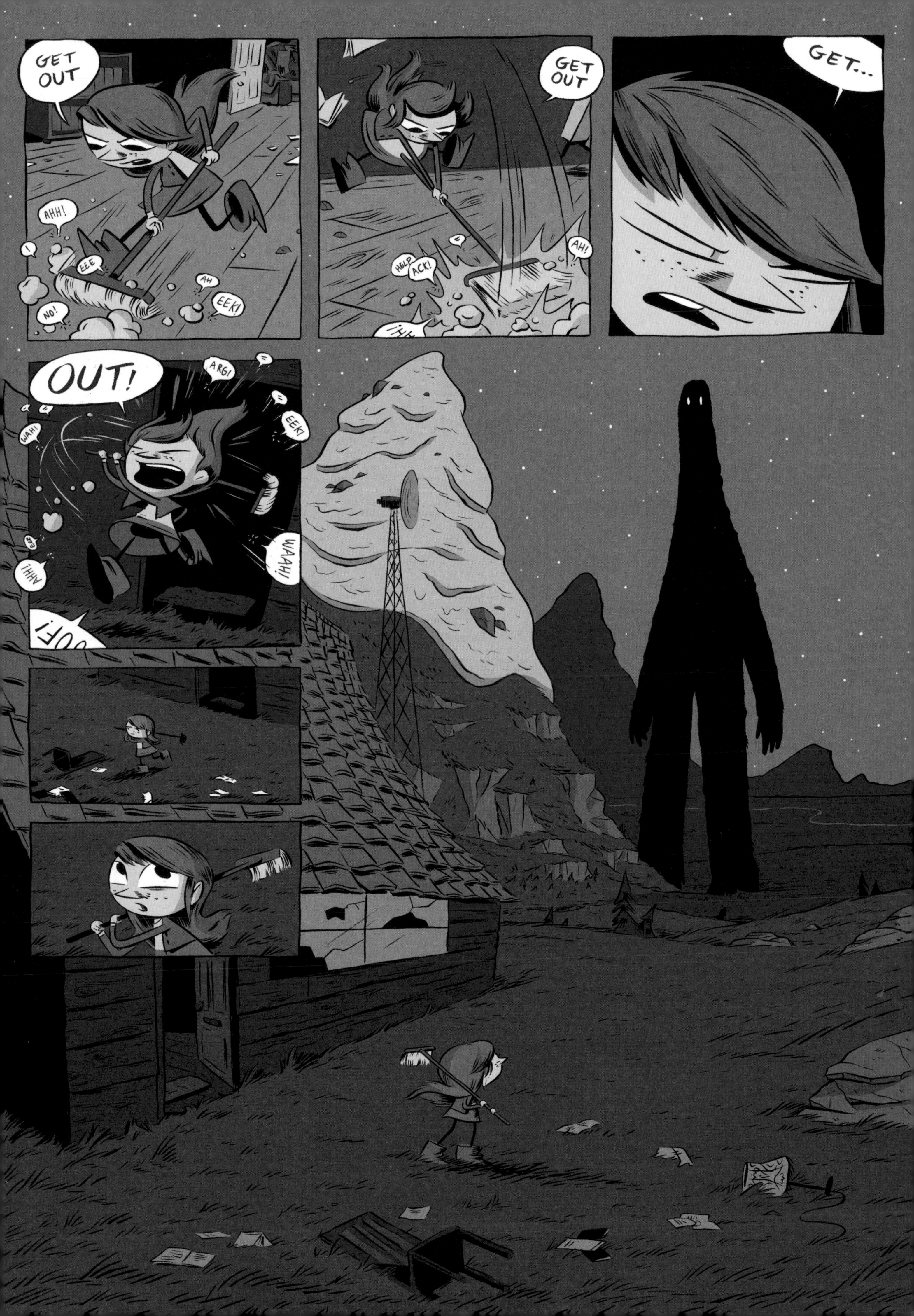
GET OUT
AHH!
EEE
AH
EEK!
NO!
GET OUT
HELP
ACK!
AH!
GET...
OUT!
ARG!
WAH!
EEK!
WAAH!
AHH!

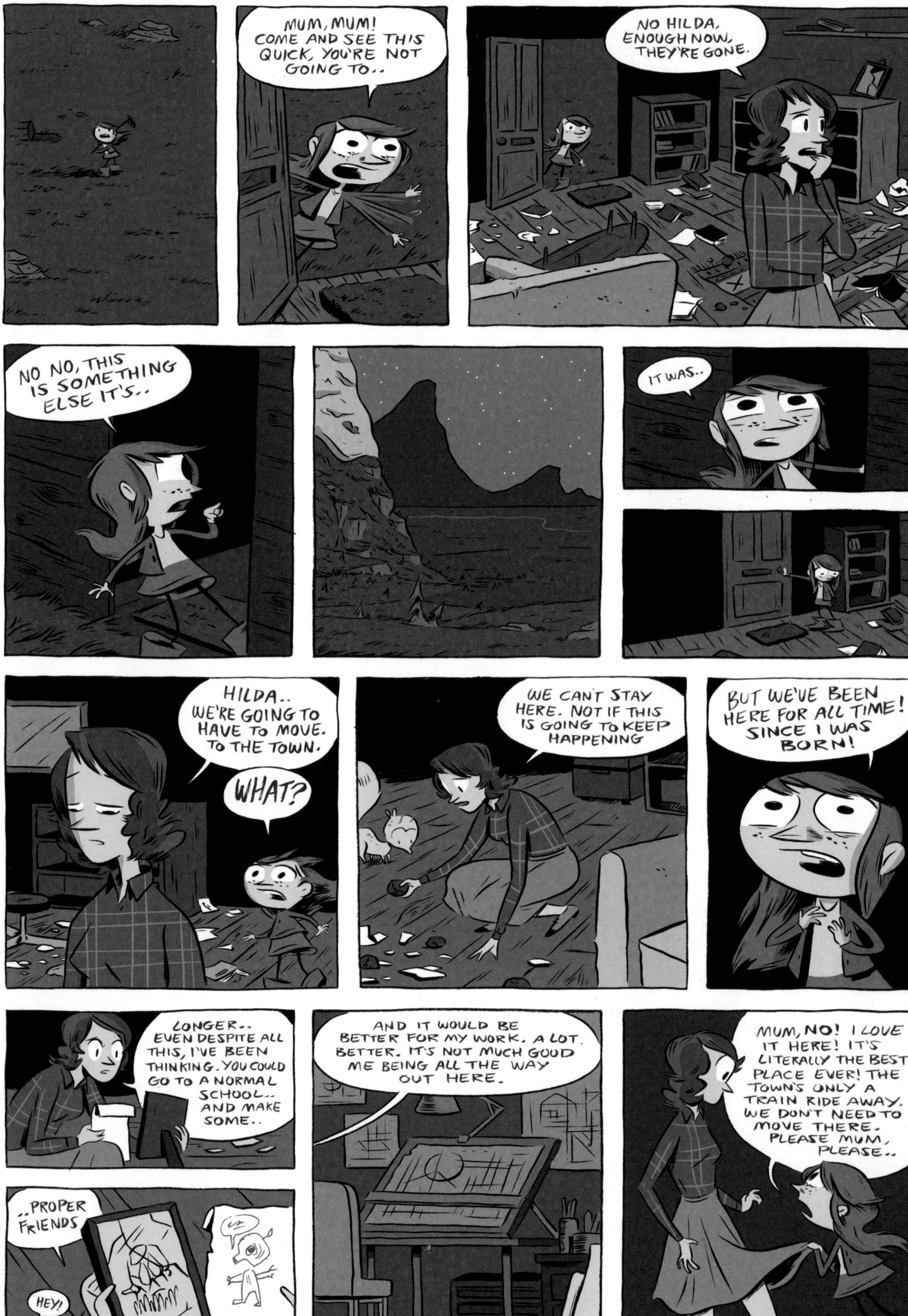
MUM, MUM! COME AND SEE THIS QUICK, YOU'RE NOT GOING TO..
NO HILDA, ENOUGH NOW, THEY'RE GONE.
NO NO, THIS IS SOMETHING ELSE IT'S..
IT WAS..
HILDA.. WE'RE GOING TO HAVE TO MOVE. TO THE TOWN.
WHAT?
WE CAN'T STAY HERE. NOT IF THIS IS GOING TO KEEP HAPPENING
BUT WE'VE BEEN HERE FOR ALL TIME! SINCE I WAS BORN!
LONGER.. EVEN DESPITE ALL THIS, I'VE BEEN THINKING. YOU COULD GO TO A NORMAL SCHOOL.. AND MAKE SOME..
..PROPER FRIENDS
HEY!
AND IT WOULD BE BETTER FOR MY WORK. A LOT BETTER. IT'S NOT MUCH GOOD ME BEING ALL THE WAY OUT HERE.
MUM, NO! I LOVE IT HERE! IT'S LITERALLY THE BEST PLACE EVER! THE TOWN'S ONLY A TRAIN RIDE AWAY. WE DON'T NEED TO MOVE THERE. PLEASE MUM, PLEASE..

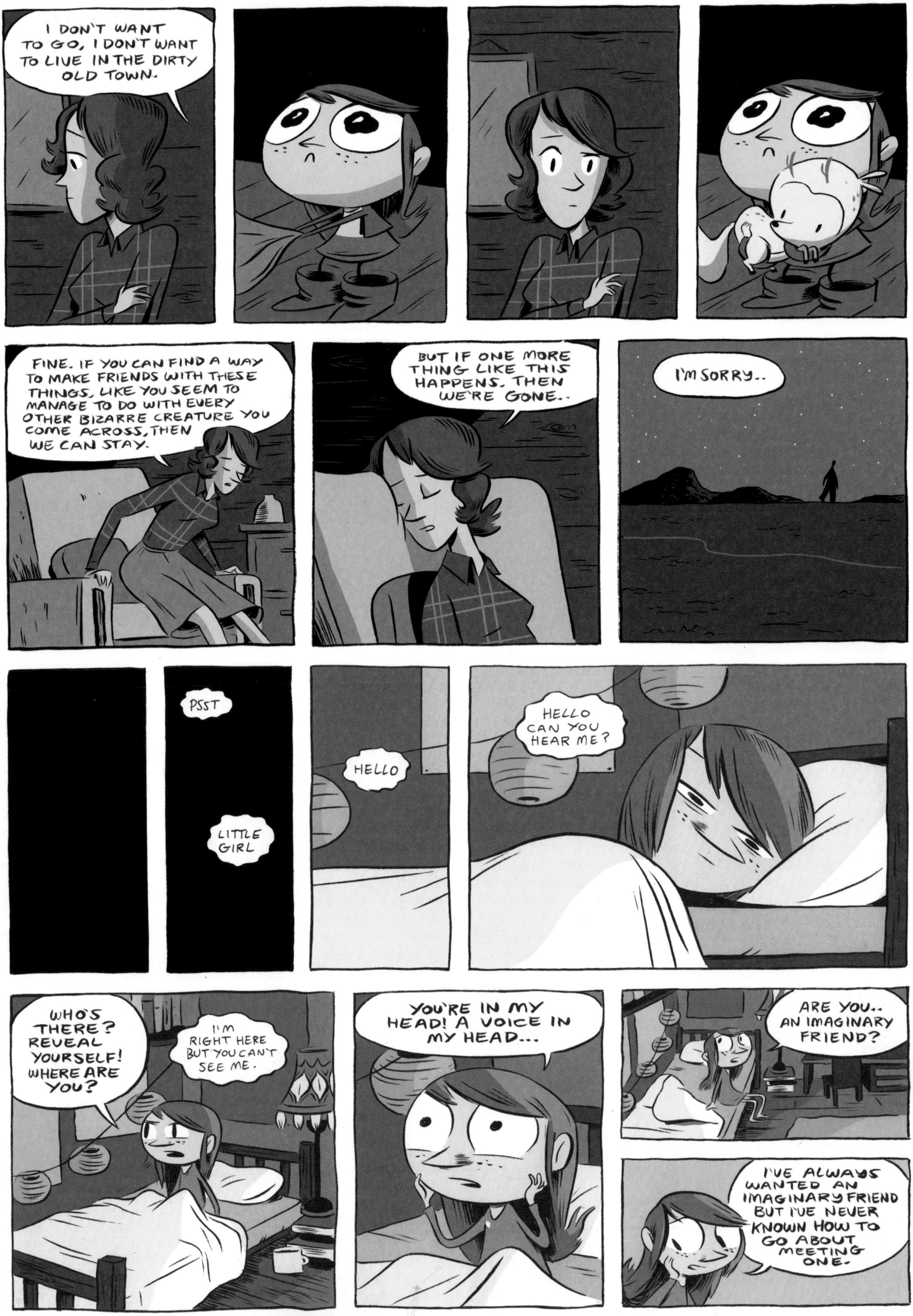
I DON'T WANT TO GO, I DON'T WANT TO LIVE IN THE DIRTY OLD TOWN.
FINE. IF YOU CAN FIND A WAY TO MAKE FRIENDS WITH THESE THINGS, LIKE YOU SEEM TO MANAGE TO DO WITH EVERY OTHER BIZARRE CREATURE YOU COME ACROSS, THEN WE CAN STAY.
BUT IF ONE MORE THING LIKE THIS HAPPENS. THEN WE'RE GONE..
I'M SORRY..
PSST
LITTLE GIRL
HELLO
HELLO CAN YOU HEAR ME?
WHO'S THERE? REVEAL YOURSELF! WHERE ARE YOU?
I'M RIGHT HERE BUT YOU CAN'T SEE ME.
YOU'RE IN MY HEAD! A VOICE IN MY HEAD...
ARE YOU.. AN IMAGINARY FRIEND?
I'VE ALWAYS WANTED AN IMAGINARY FRIEND BUT I'VE NEVER KNOWN HOW TO GO ABOUT MEETING ONE.

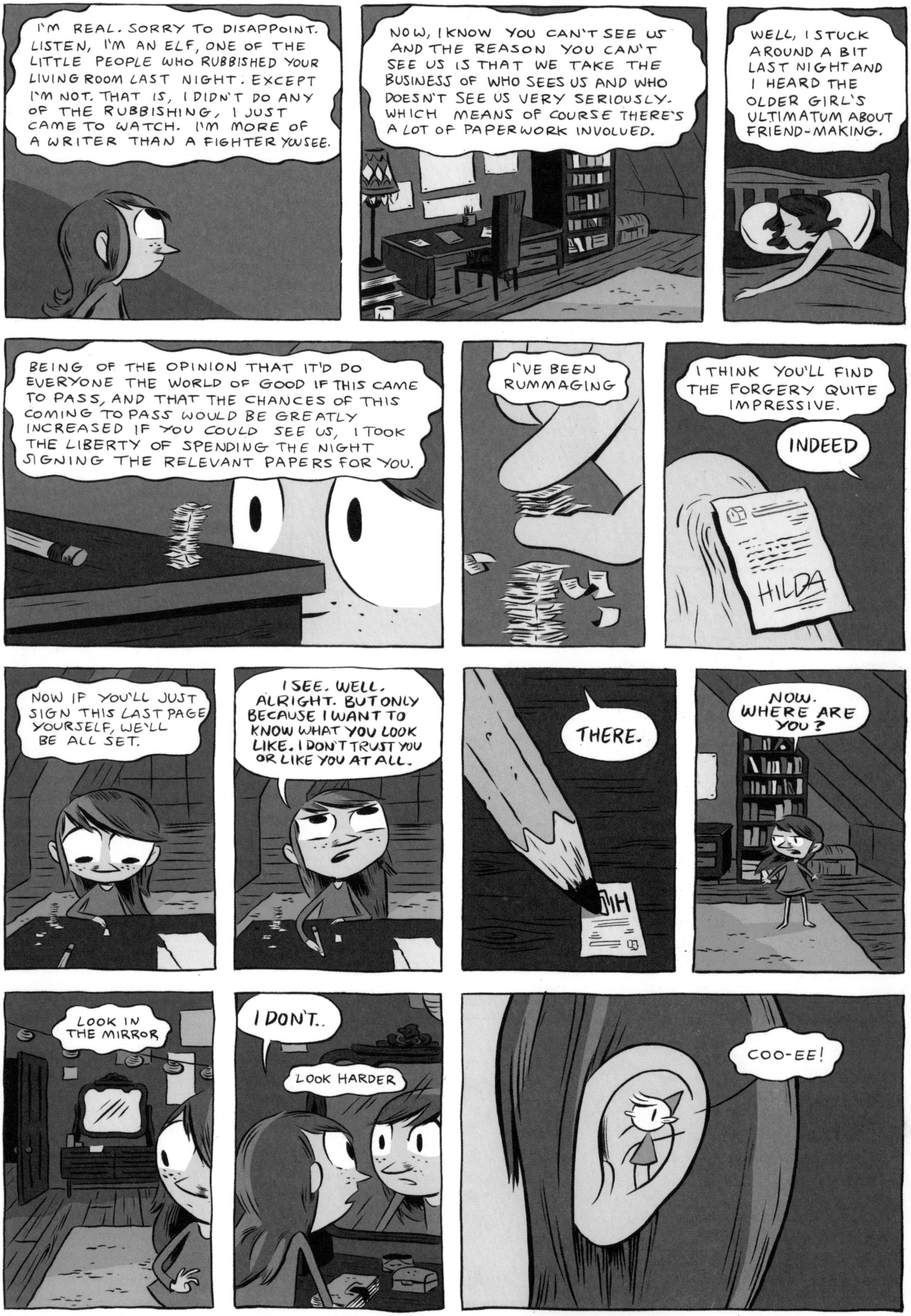
I'M REAL. SORRY TO DISAPPOINT. LISTEN, I'M AN ELF, ONE OF THE LITTLE PEOPLE WHO RUBBISHED YOUR LIVING ROOM LAST NIGHT. EXCEPT I'M NOT. THAT IS, I DIDN'T DO ANY OF THE RUBBISHING, I JUST CAME TO WATCH. I'M MORE OF A WRITER THAN A FIGHTER YOU SEE.
NOW, I KNOW YOU CAN'T SEE US AND THE REASON YOU CAN'T SEE US IS THAT WE TAKE THE BUSINESS OF WHO SEES US AND WHO DOESN'T SEE US VERY SERIOUSLY. WHICH MEANS OF COURSE THERE'S A LOT OF PAPERWORK INVOLVED.
WELL, I STUCK AROUND A BIT LAST NIGHT AND I HEARD THE OLDER GIRL'S ULTIMATUM ABOUT FRIEND-MAKING.
BEING OF THE OPINION THAT IT'D DO EVERYONE THE WORLD OF GOOD IF THIS CAME TO PASS, AND THAT THE CHANCES OF THIS COMING TO PASS WOULD BE GREATLY INCREASED IF YOU COULD SEE US, I TOOK THE LIBERTY OF SPENDING THE NIGHT SIGNING THE RELEVANT PAPERS FOR YOU.
I'VE BEEN RUMMAGING
I THINK YOU'LL FIND THE FORGERY QUITE IMPRESSIVE.
INDEED
HILDA
NOW IF YOU'LL JUST SIGN THIS LAST PAGE YOURSELF, WE'LL BE ALL SET.
I SEE. WELL. ALRIGHT. BUT ONLY BECAUSE I WANT TO KNOW WHAT YOU LOOK LIKE. I DON'T TRUST YOU OR LIKE YOU AT ALL.
THERE.
NOW. WHERE ARE YOU?
LOOK IN THE MIRROR
I DON'T..
LOOK HARDER
COO-EE!

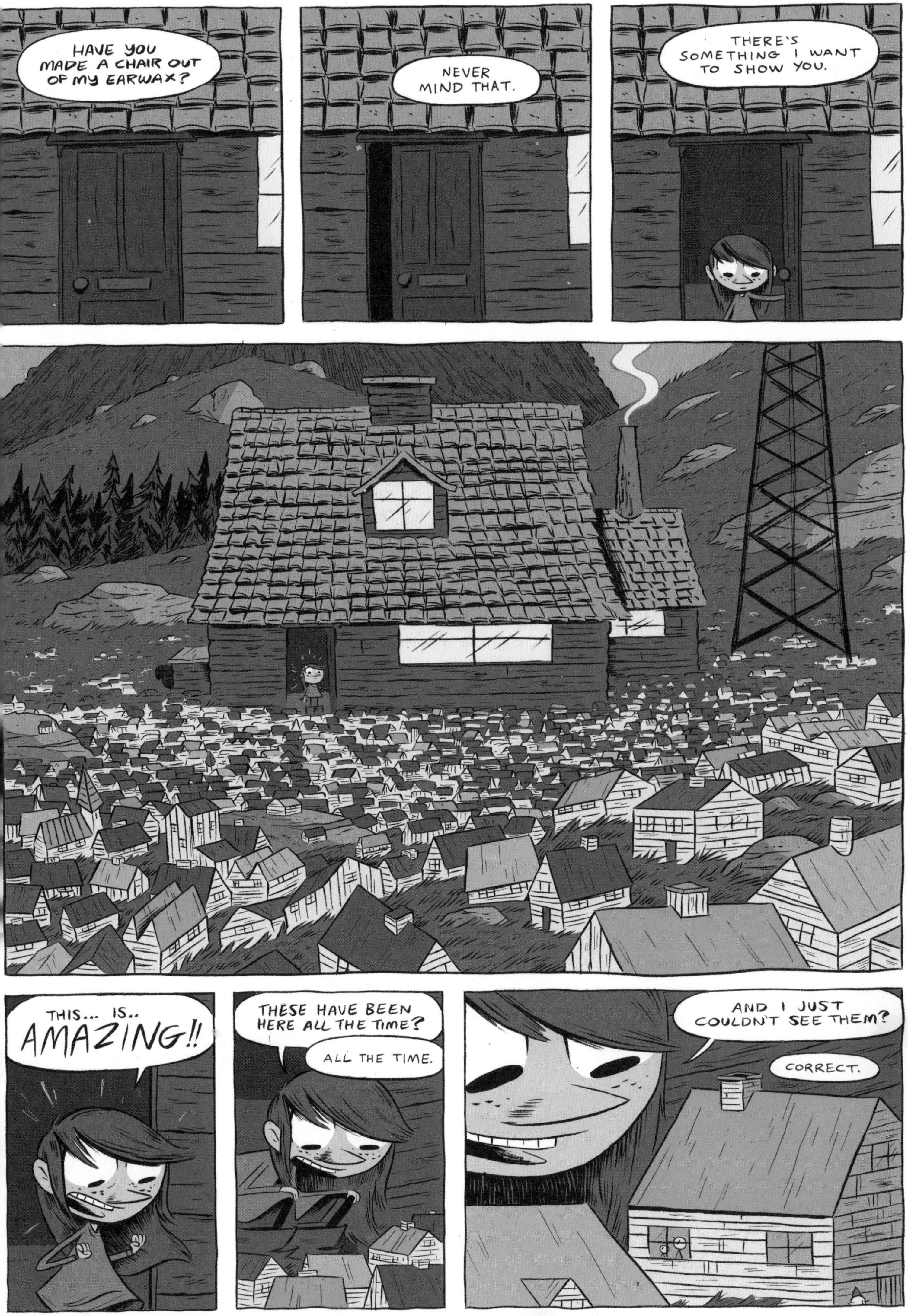
HAVE YOU MADE A CHAIR OUT OF MY EARWAX?
NEVER MIND THAT.
THERE'S SOMETHING I WANT TO SHOW YOU.
THIS... IS.. AMAZING!!
THESE HAVE BEEN HERE ALL THE TIME?
ALL THE TIME.
AND I JUST COULDN'T SEE THEM?
CORRECT.

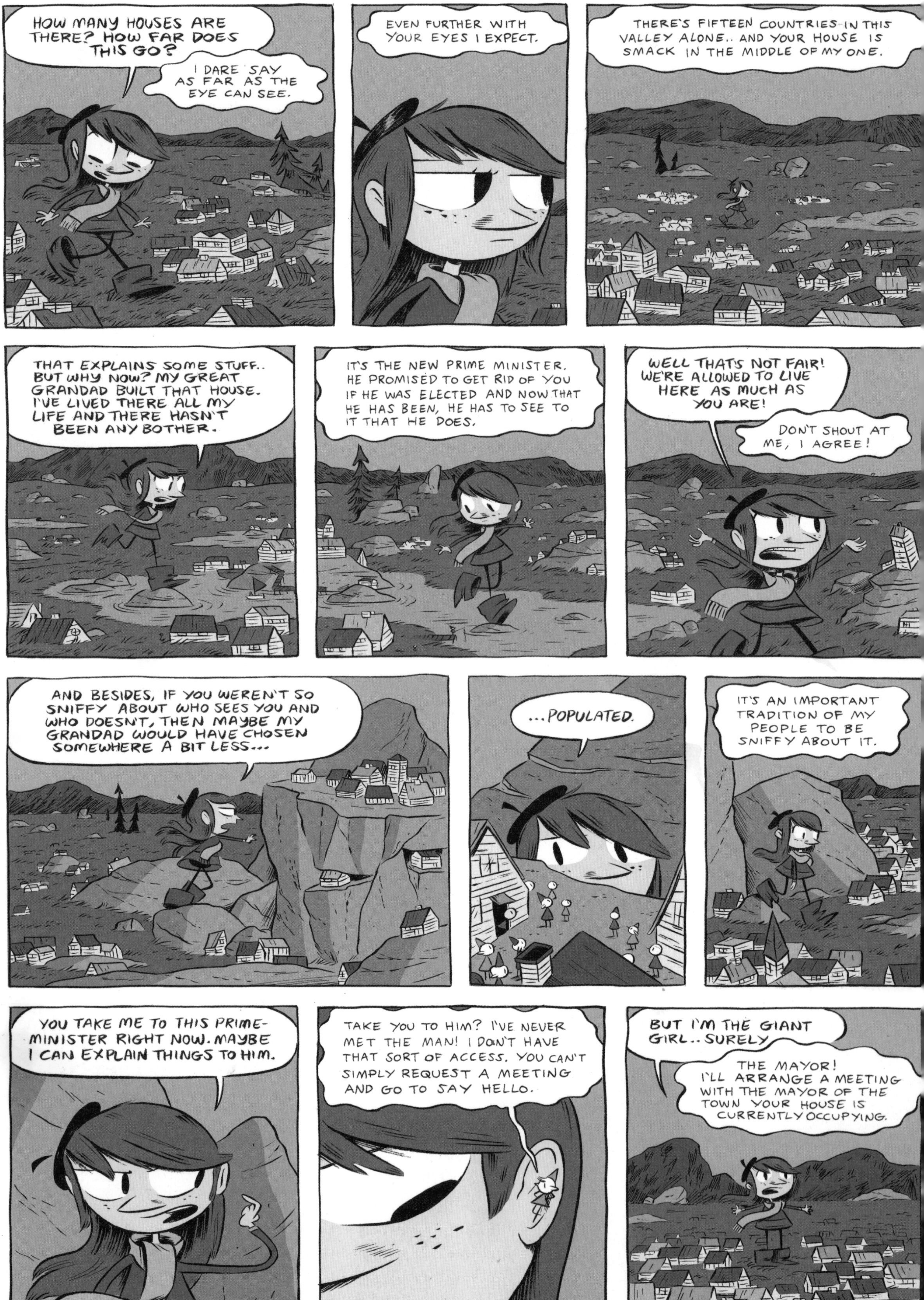
HOW MANY HOUSES ARE THERE? HOW FAR DOES THIS GO?
I DARE SAY AS FAR AS THE EYE CAN SEE.
EVEN FURTHER WITH YOUR EYES I EXPECT.
THERE'S FIFTEEN COUNTRIES IN THIS VALLEY ALONE.. AND YOUR HOUSE IS SMACK IN THE MIDDLE OF MY ONE.
THAT EXPLAINS SOME STUFF.. BUT WHY NOW? MY GREAT GRANDAD BUILT THAT HOUSE. I'VE LIVED THERE ALL MY LIFE AND THERE HASN'T BEEN ANY BOTHER.
IT'S THE NEW PRIME MINISTER. HE PROMISED TO GET RID OF YOU IF HE WAS ELECTED AND NOW THAT HE HAS BEEN, HE HAS TO SEE TO IT THAT HE DOES.
WELL THAT'S NOT FAIR! WE'RE ALLOWED TO LIVE HERE AS MUCH AS YOU ARE!
DON'T SHOUT AT ME, I AGREE!
AND BESIDES, IF YOU WEREN'T SO SNIFFY ABOUT WHO SEES YOU AND WHO DOESN'T, THEN MAYBE MY GRANDAD WOULD HAVE CHOSEN SOMEWHERE A BIT LESS...
...POPULATED.
IT'S AN IMPORTANT TRADITION OF MY PEOPLE TO BE SNIFFY ABOUT IT.
YOU TAKE ME TO THIS PRIME-MINISTER RIGHT NOW. MAYBE I CAN EXPLAIN THINGS TO HIM.
TAKE YOU TO HIM? I'VE NEVER MET THE MAN! I DON'T HAVE THAT SORT OF ACCESS. YOU CAN'T SIMPLY REQUEST A MEETING AND GO TO SAY HELLO.
BUT I'M THE GIANT GIRL.. SURELY
THE MAYOR! I'LL ARRANGE A MEETING WITH THE MAYOR OF THE TOWN YOUR HOUSE IS CURRENTLY OCCUPYING.

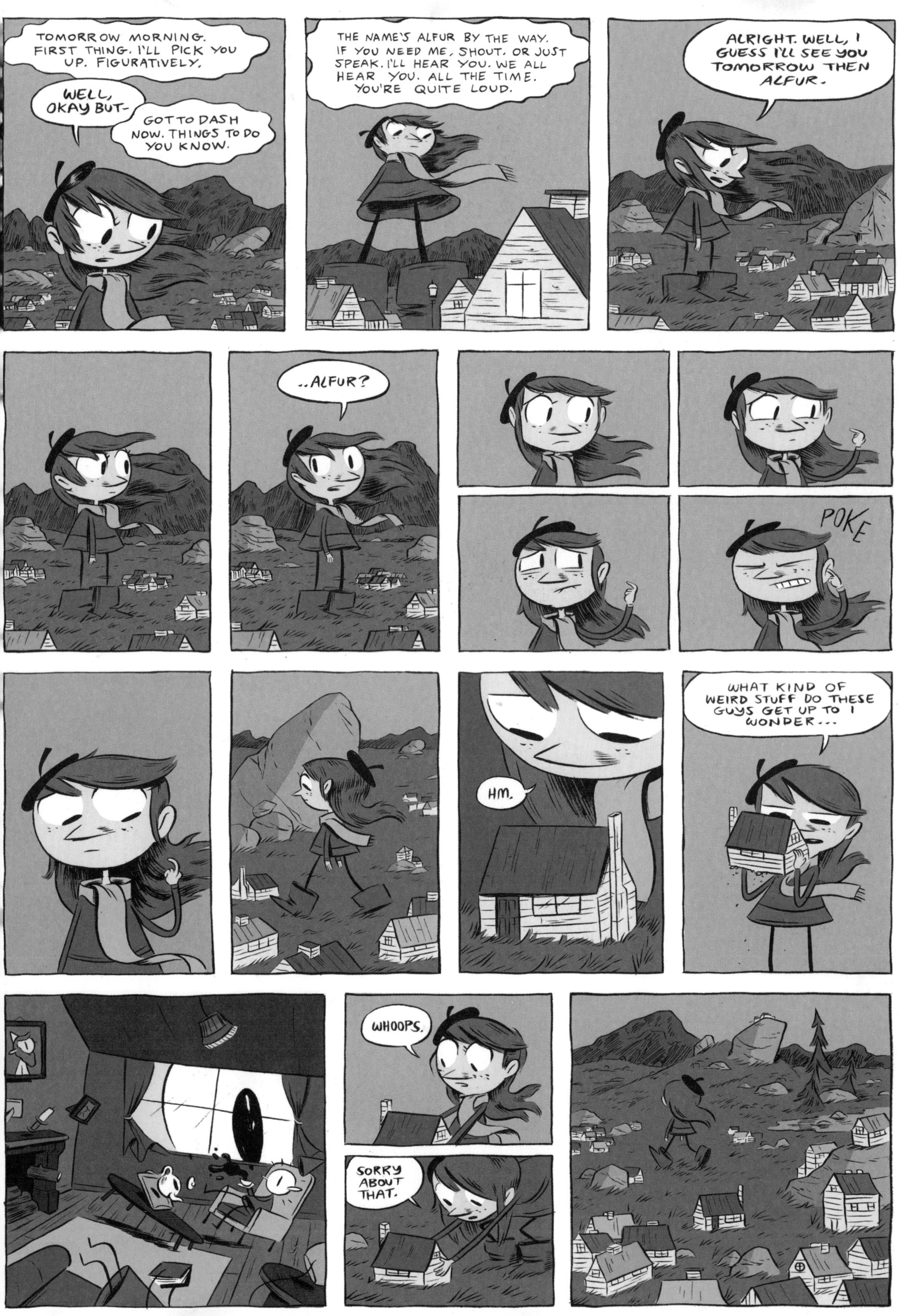
TOMORROW MORNING. FIRST THING. I'LL PICK YOU UP. FIGURATIVELY.
WELL, OKAY BUT-
GOT TO DASH NOW. THINGS TO DO YOU KNOW.
THE NAME'S ALFUR BY THE WAY. IF YOU NEED ME, SHOUT, OR JUST SPEAK. I'LL HEAR YOU. WE ALL HEAR YOU. ALL THE TIME. YOU'RE QUITE LOUD.
ALRIGHT. WELL, I GUESS I'LL SEE YOU TOMORROW THEN ALFUR.
..ALFUR?
POKE
HM.
WHAT KIND OF WEIRD STUFF DO THESE GUYS GET UP TO I WONDER...
WHOOPS.
SORRY ABOUT THAT.

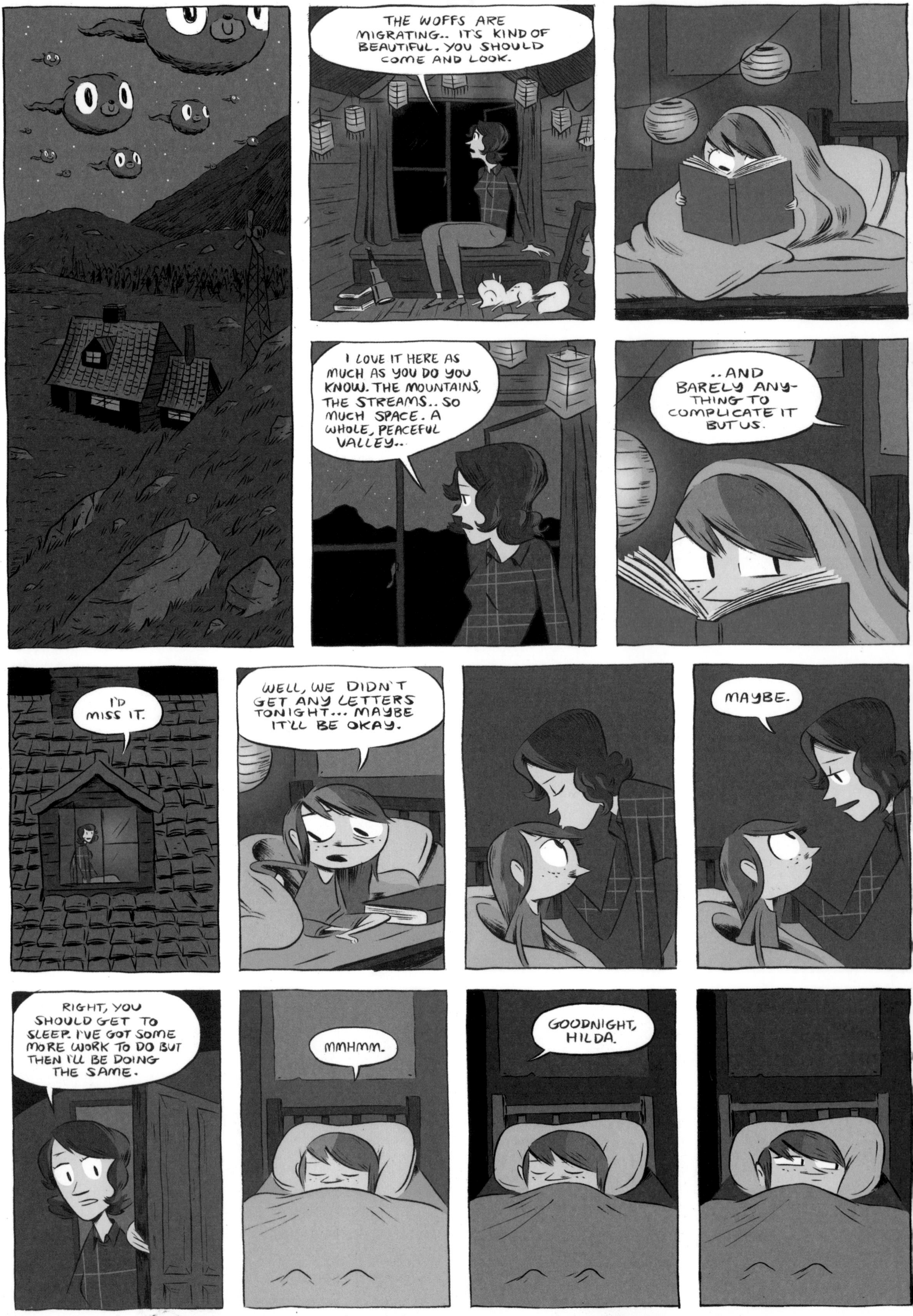
THE WOFFS ARE MIGRATING.. IT'S KIND OF BEAUTIFUL. YOU SHOULD COME AND LOOK.
I LOVE IT HERE AS MUCH AS YOU DO YOU KNOW. THE MOUNTAINS, THE STREAMS.. SO MUCH SPACE. A WHOLE, PEACEFUL VALLEY..
..AND BARELY ANYTHING TO COMPLICATE IT BUT US.
I'D MISS IT.
WELL, WE DIDN'T GET ANY LETTERS TONIGHT... MAYBE IT'LL BE OKAY.
MAYBE.
RIGHT, YOU SHOULD GET TO SLEEP. I'VE GOT SOME MORE WORK TO DO BUT THEN I'LL BE DOING THE SAME.
MMHMM.
GOODNIGHT, HILDA.

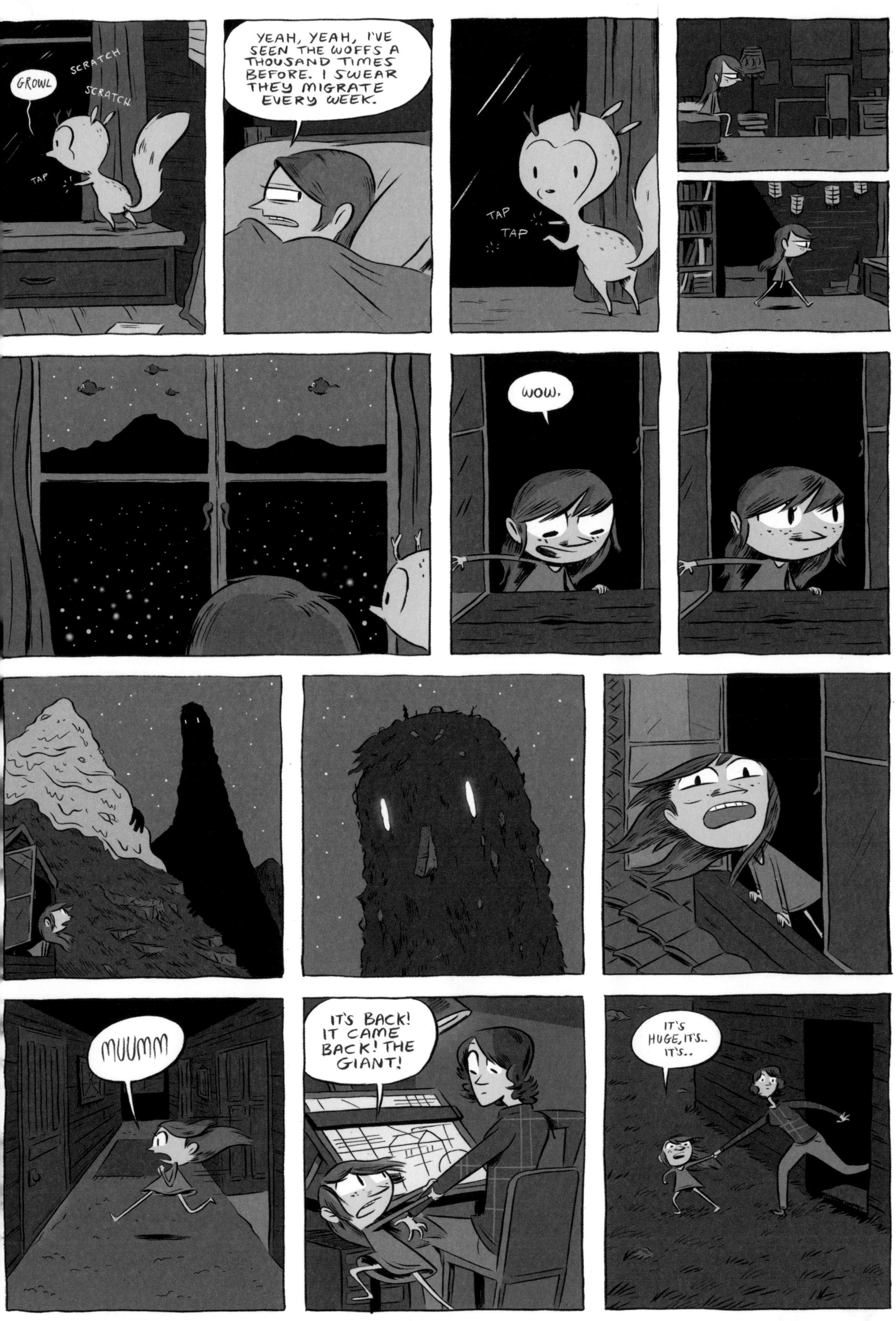
GROWL
SCRATCH
SCRATCH
TAP
YEAH, YEAH, I'VE SEEN THE WOFFS A THOUSAND TIMES BEFORE. I SWEAR THEY MIGRATE EVERY WEEK.
TAP
TAP
WOW.
MUUMM
IT'S BACK! IT CAME BACK! THE GIANT!
IT'S HUGE, IT'S.. IT'S..

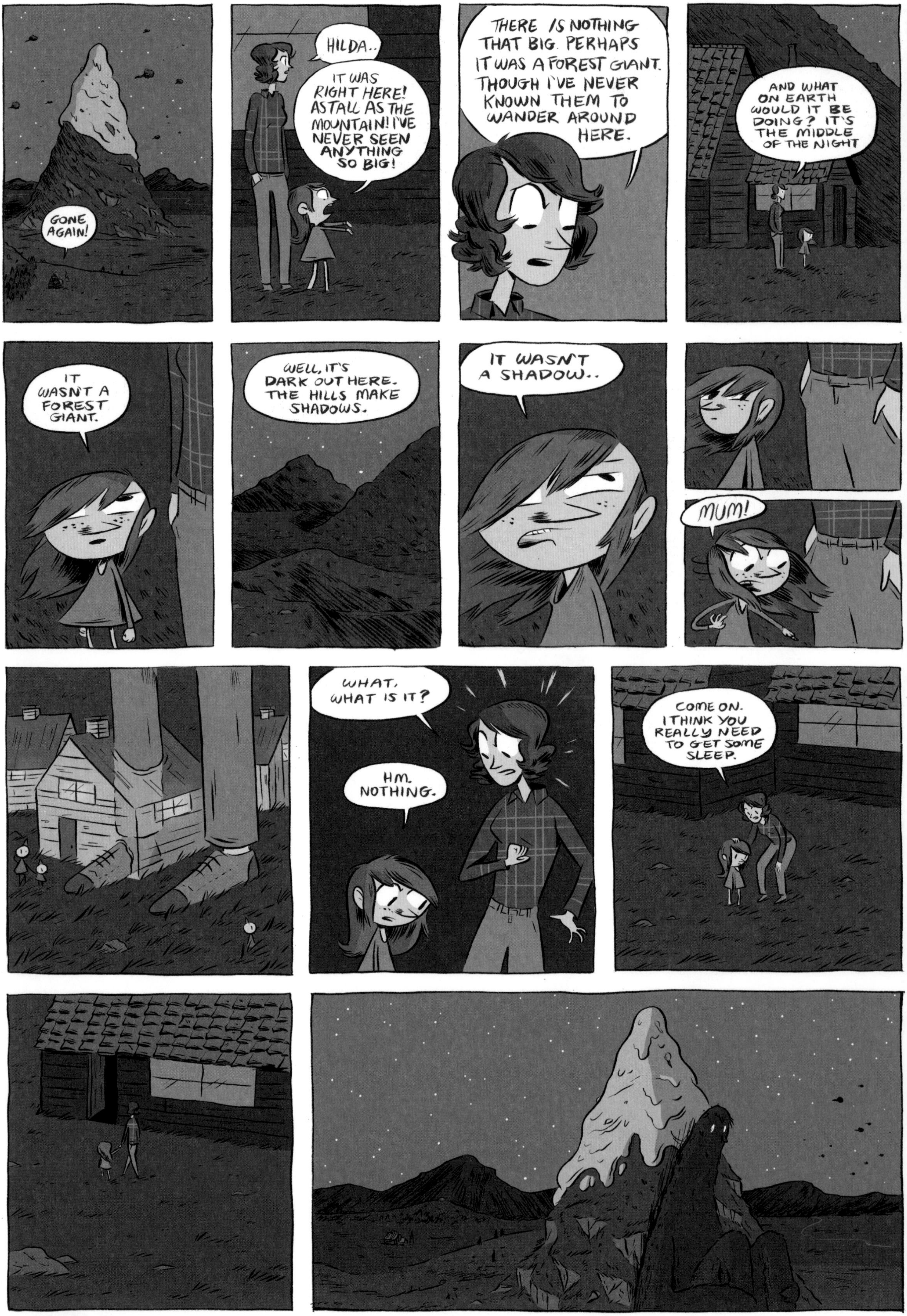
GONE AGAIN!
HILDA..
IT WAS RIGHT HERE! AS TALL AS THE MOUNTAIN! I'VE NEVER SEEN ANYTHING SO BIG!
THERE IS NOTHING THAT BIG. PERHAPS IT WAS A FOREST GIANT. THOUGH I'VE NEVER KNOWN THEM TO WANDER AROUND HERE.
AND WHAT ON EARTH WOULD IT BE DOING? IT'S THE MIDDLE OF THE NIGHT
IT WASN'T A FOREST GIANT.
WELL, IT'S DARK OUT HERE. THE HILLS MAKE SHADOWS.
IT WASN'T A SHADOW..
MUM!
WHAT, WHAT IS IT?
HM. NOTHING.
COME ON. I THINK YOU REALLY NEED TO GET SOME SLEEP.

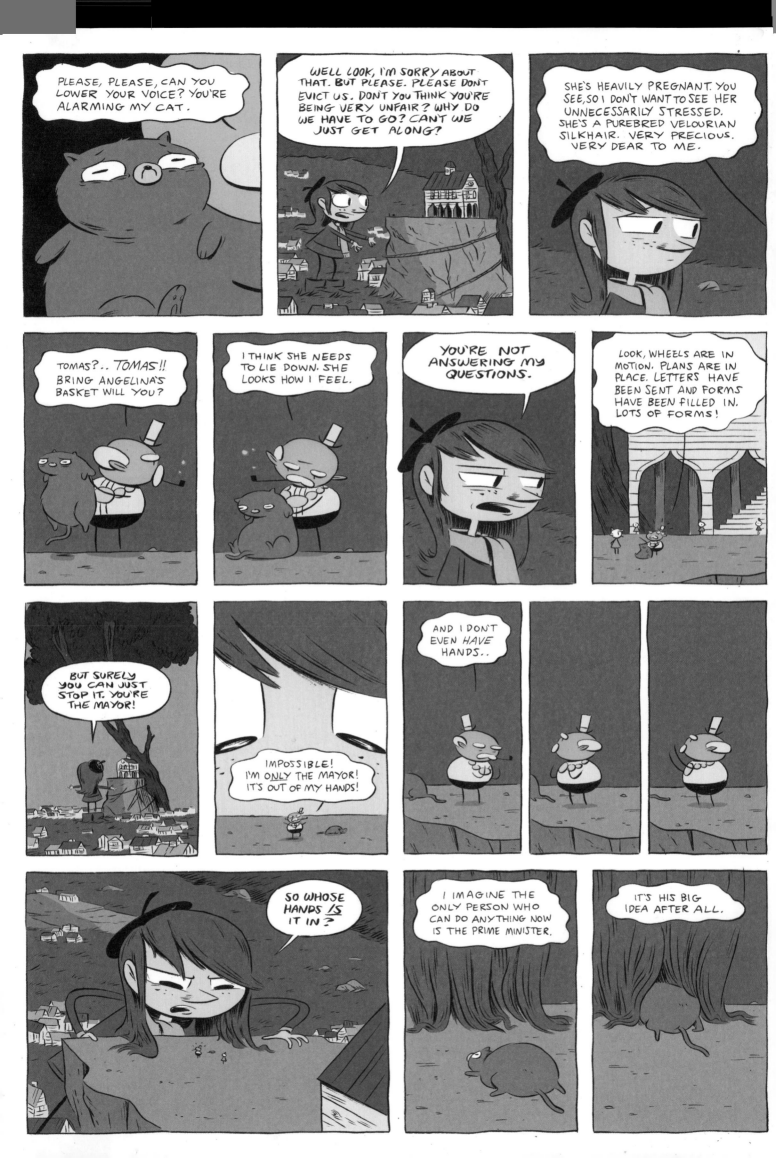

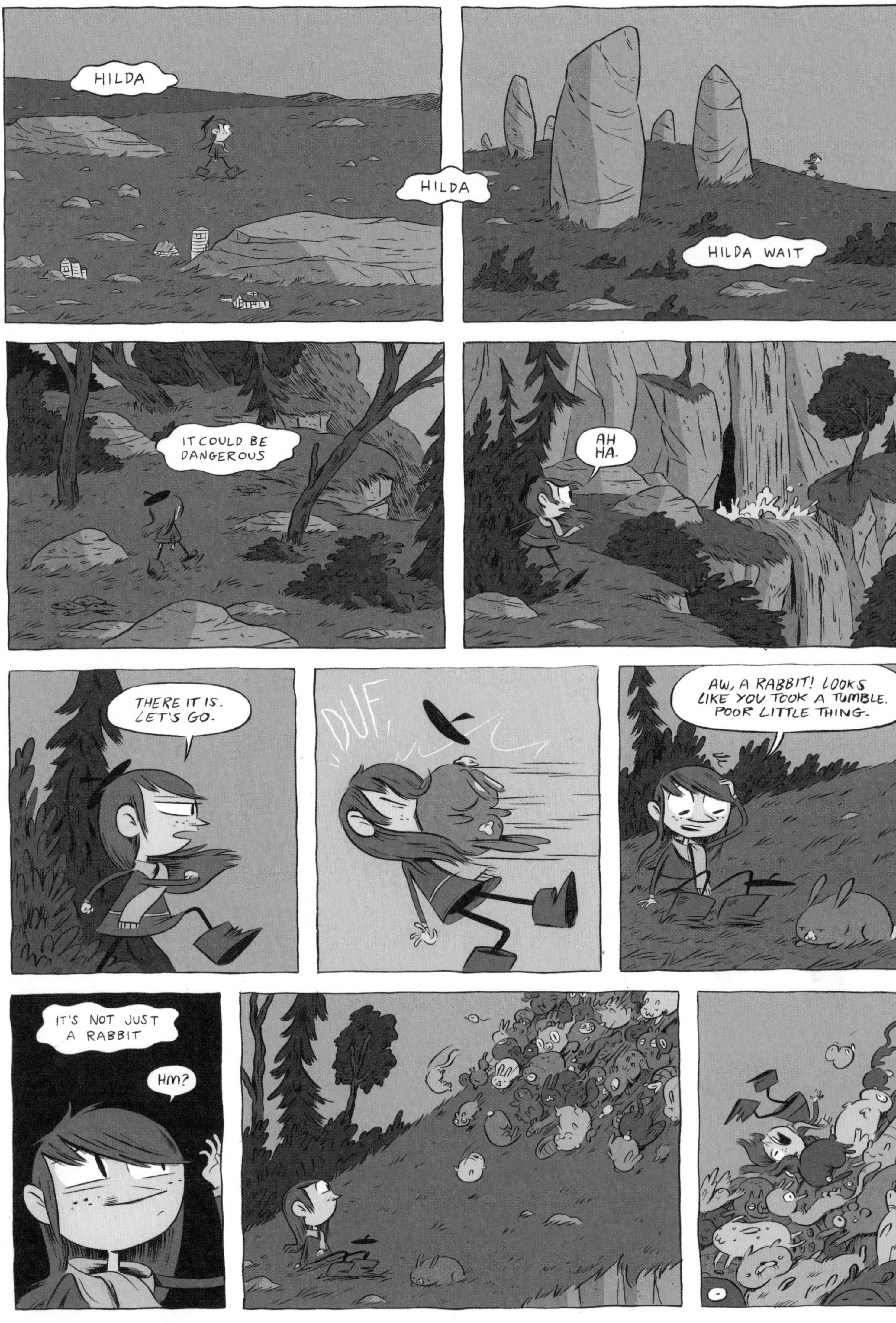
HILDA
HILDA
HILDA WAIT
IT COULD BE DANGEROUS
AH HA.
THERE IT IS. LET'S GO.
DUF,
AW, A RABBIT! LOOKS LIKE YOU TOOK A TUMBLE. POOR LITTLE THING.
IT'S NOT JUST A RABBIT
Hm?

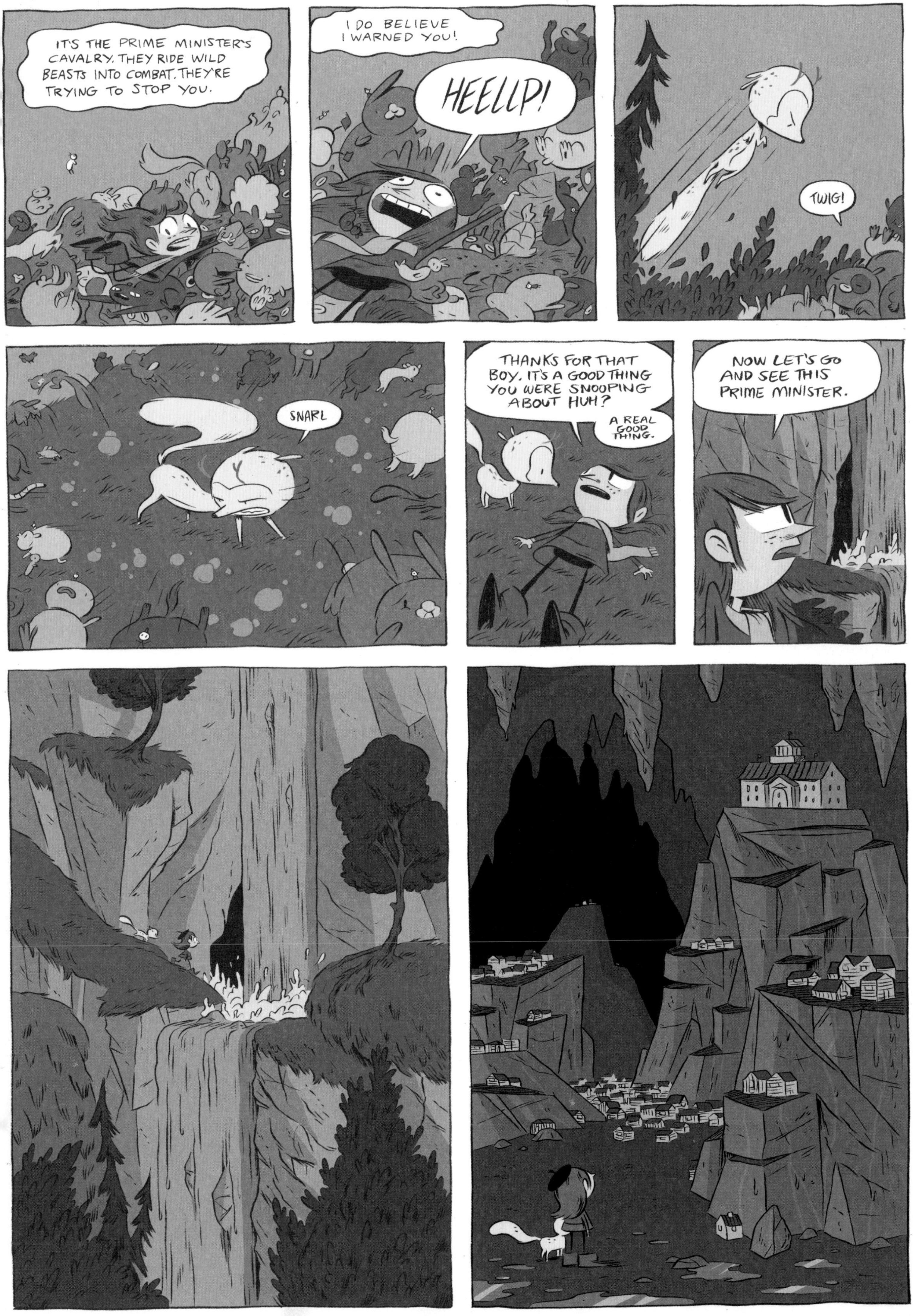
IT'S THE PRIME MINISTER'S CAVALRY. THEY RIDE WILD BEASTS INTO COMBAT. THEY'RE TRYING TO STOP YOU.
I DO BELIEVE I WARNED YOU!
HEELLP!
TWIG!
SNARL
THANKS FOR THAT BOY. IT'S A GOOD THING YOU WERE SNOOPING ABOUT HUH?
A REAL GOOD THING.
NOW LET'S GO AND SEE THIS PRIME MINISTER.

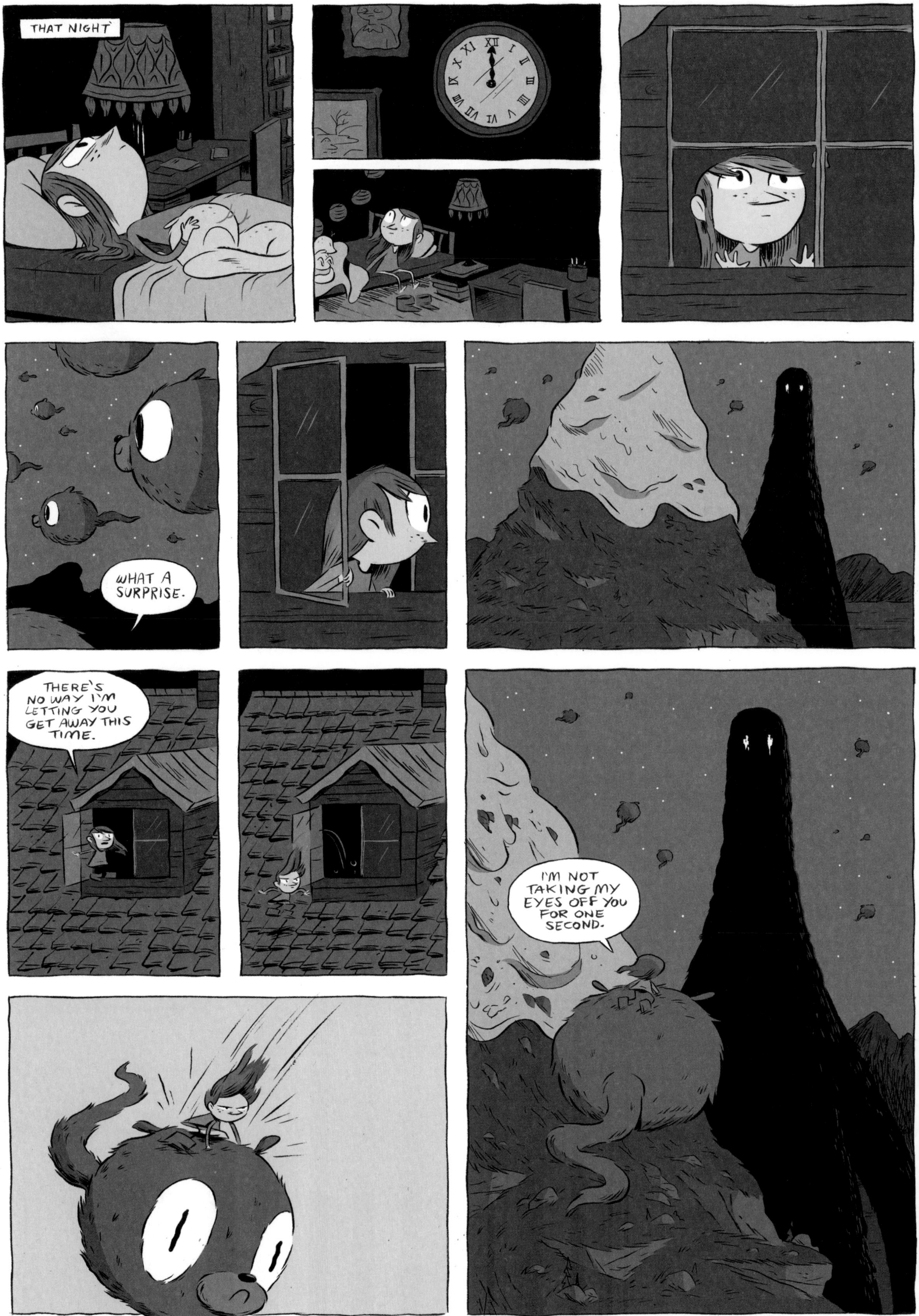
THAT NIGHT
WHAT A SURPRISE.
THERE'S NO WAY I'M LETTING YOU GET AWAY THIS TIME.
I'M NOT TAKING MY EYES OFF YOU FOR ONE SECOND.

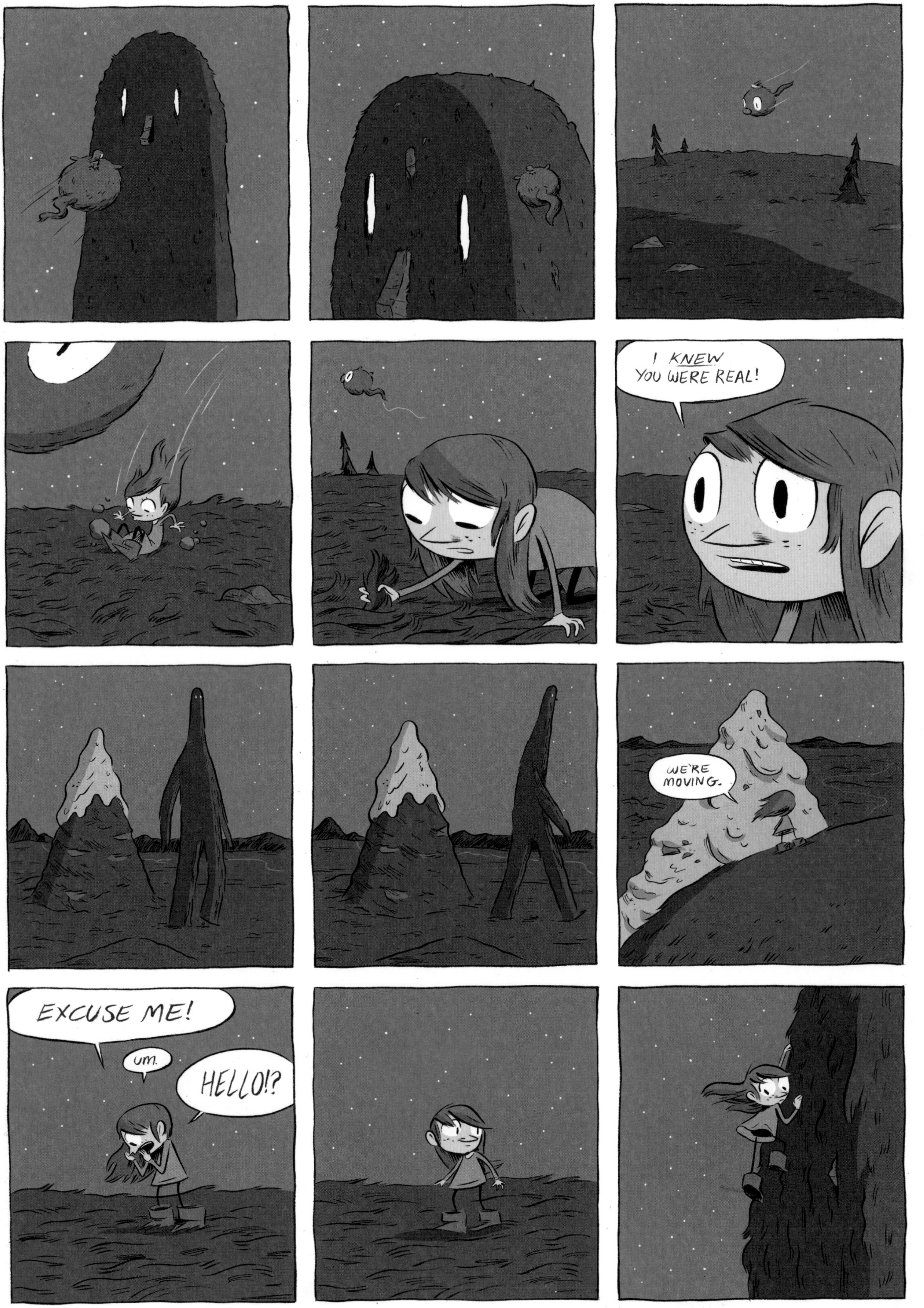
I KNEW YOU WERE REAL!
WE'RE MOVING.
EXCUSE ME!
um.
HELLO!?

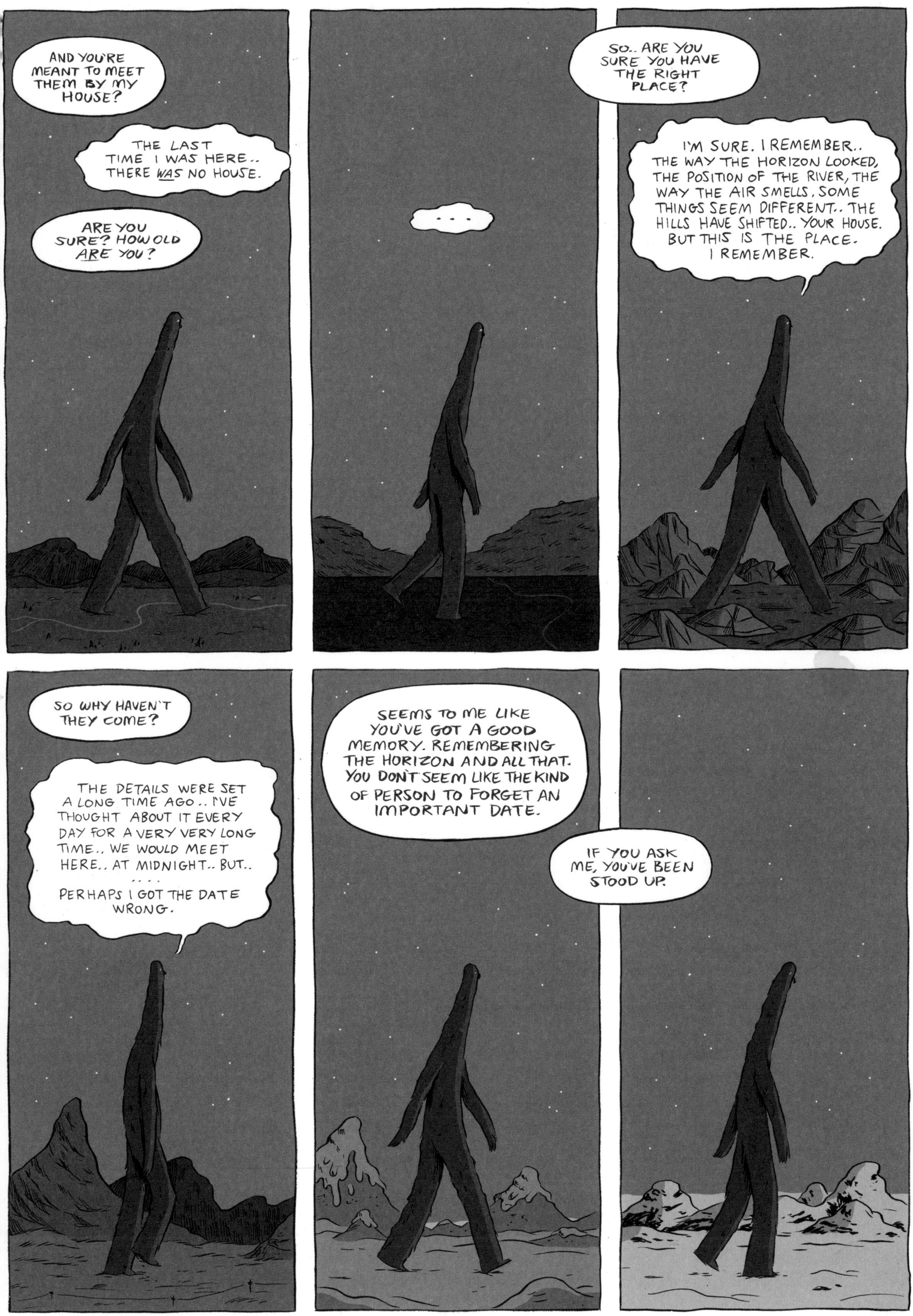
AND YOU'RE MEANT TO MEET THEM BY MY HOUSE?
THE LAST TIME I WAS HERE.. THERE WAS NO HOUSE.
ARE YOU SURE? HOW OLD ARE YOU?
...
SO.. ARE YOU SURE YOU HAVE THE RIGHT PLACE?
I'M SURE. I REMEMBER.. THE WAY THE HORIZON LOOKED, THE POSITION OF THE RIVER, THE WAY THE AIR SMELLS. SOME THINGS SEEM DIFFERENT.. THE HILLS HAVE SHIFTED.. YOUR HOUSE. BUT THIS IS THE PLACE. I REMEMBER.
SO WHY HAVEN'T THEY COME?
THE DETAILS WERE SET A LONG TIME AGO.. I'VE THOUGHT ABOUT IT EVERY DAY FOR A VERY VERY LONG TIME.. WE WOULD MEET HERE.. AT MIDNIGHT.. BUT.. .... PERHAPS I GOT THE DATE WRONG.
SEEMS TO ME LIKE YOU'VE GOT A GOOD MEMORY. REMEMBERING THE HORIZON AND ALL THAT. YOU DON'T SEEM LIKE THE KIND OF PERSON TO FORGET AN IMPORTANT DATE.
IF YOU ASK ME, YOU'VE BEEN STOOD UP.

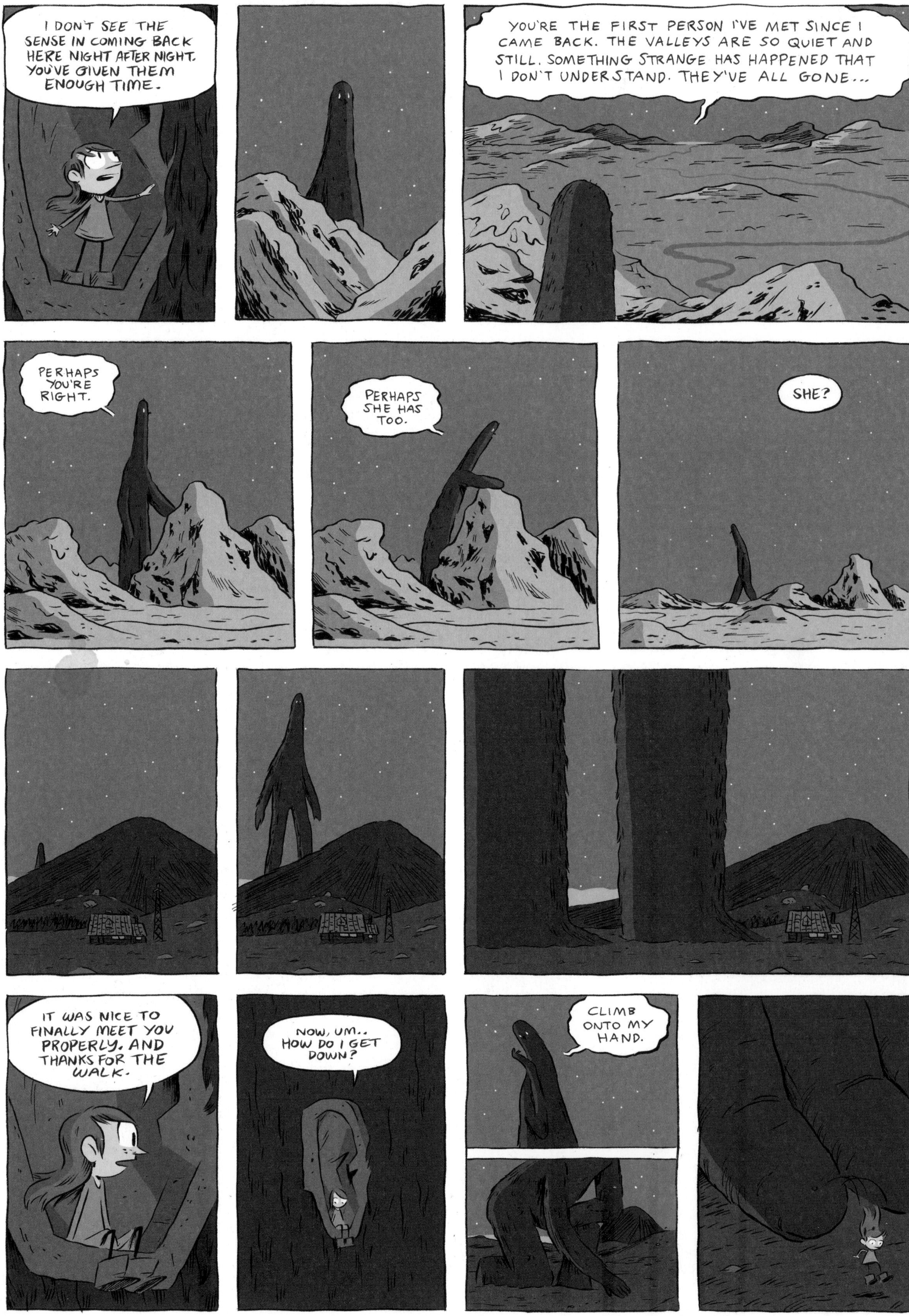
I DON'T SEE THE SENSE IN COMING BACK HERE NIGHT AFTER NIGHT. YOU'VE GIVEN THEM ENOUGH TIME.
YOU'RE THE FIRST PERSON I'VE MET SINCE I CAME BACK. THE VALLEYS ARE SO QUIET AND STILL. SOMETHING STRANGE HAS HAPPENED THAT I DON'T UNDERSTAND. THEY'VE ALL GONE...
PERHAPS YOU'RE RIGHT.
PERHAPS SHE HAS TOO.
SHE?
IT WAS NICE TO FINALLY MEET YOU PROPERLY. AND THANKS FOR THE WALK.
NOW, UM.. HOW DO I GET DOWN?
CLIMB ONTO MY HAND.

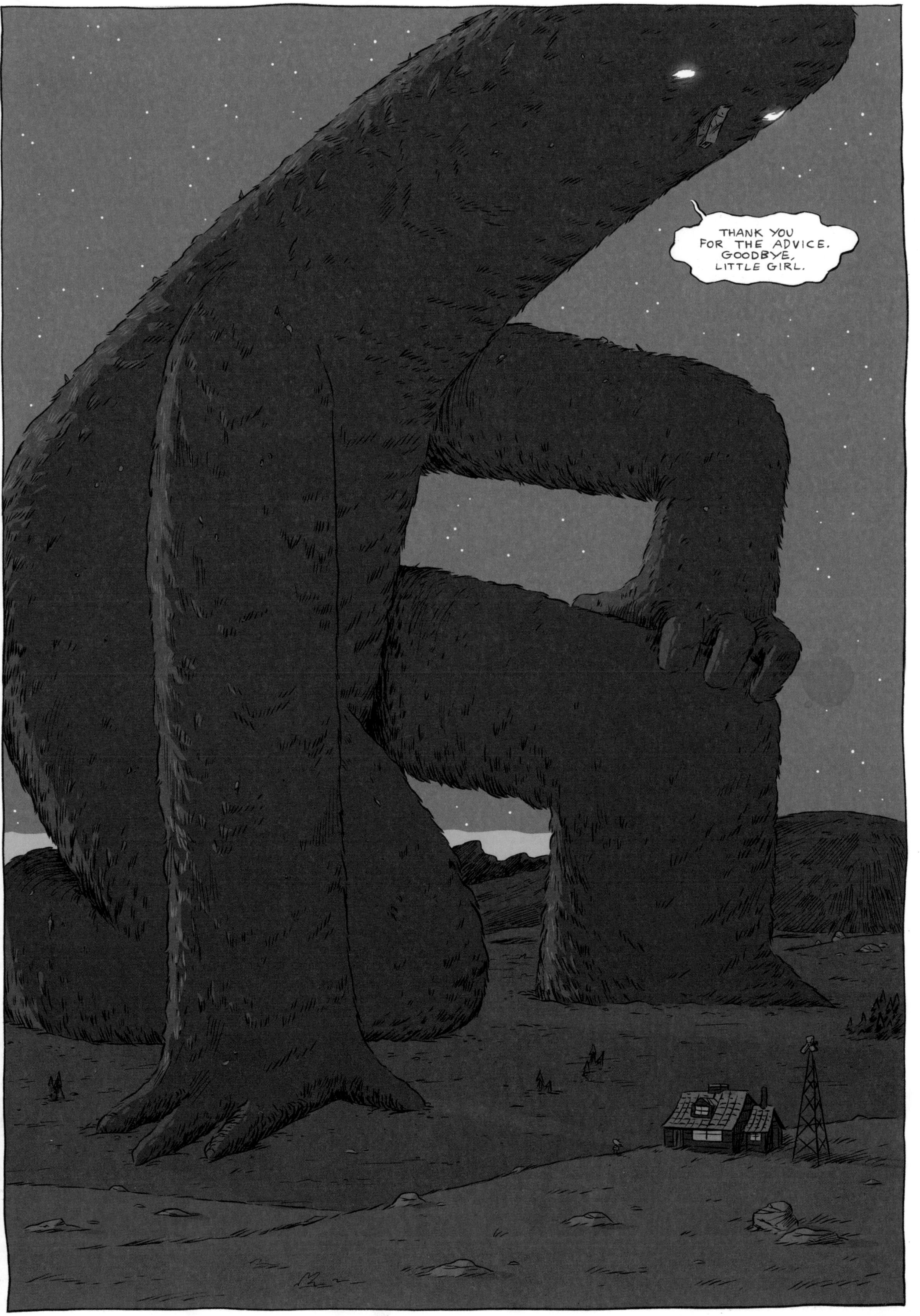
THANK YOU FOR THE ADVICE. GOODBYE, LITTLE GIRL.

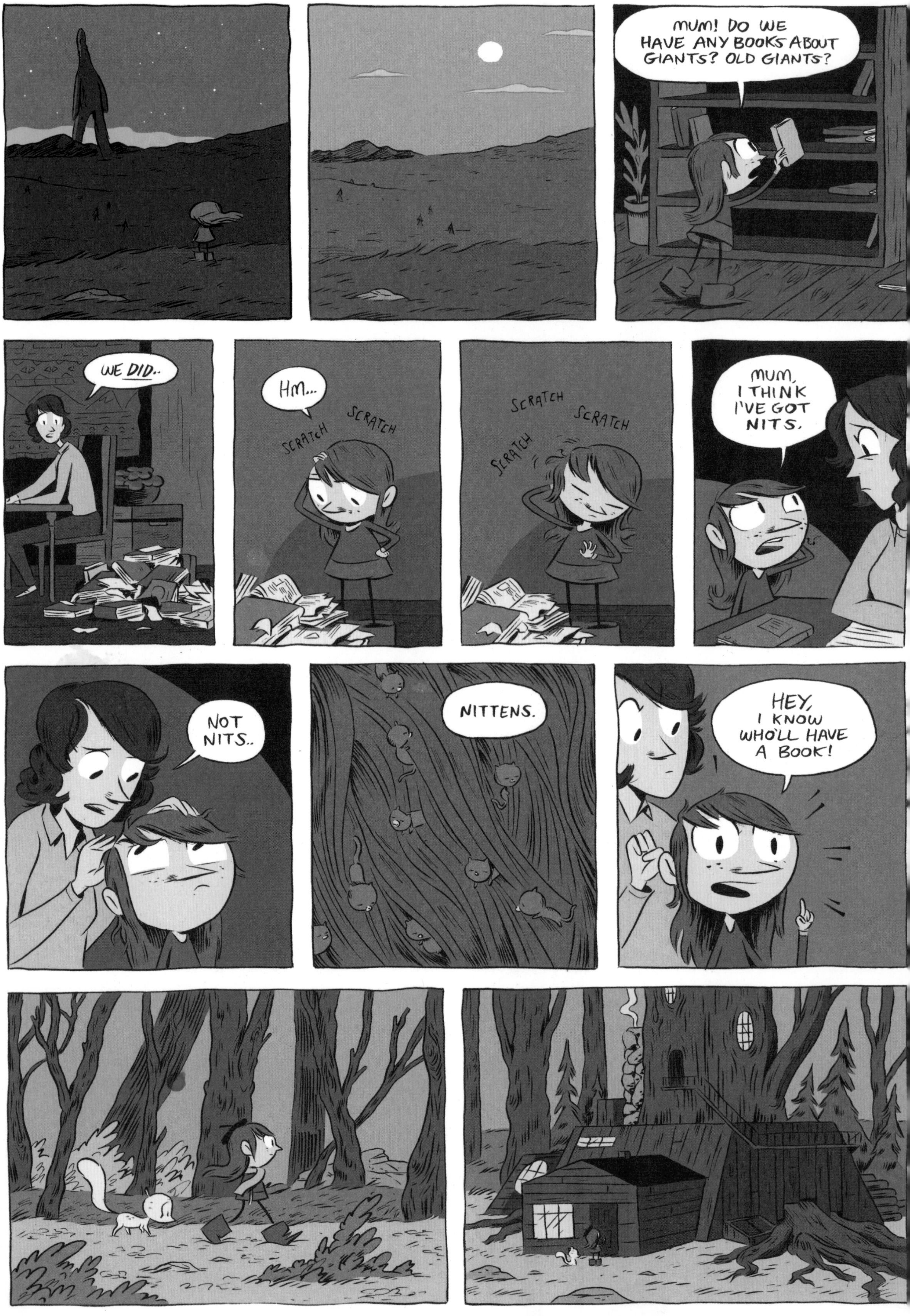
MUM! DO WE HAVE ANY BOOKS ABOUT GIANTS? OLD GIANTS?
WE DID..
HM...
SCRATCH
SCRATCH
SCRATCH
SCRATCH
SCRATCH
MUM, I THINK I'VE GOT NITS.
NOT NITS..
NITTENS.
HEY, I KNOW WHO'LL HAVE A BOOK!

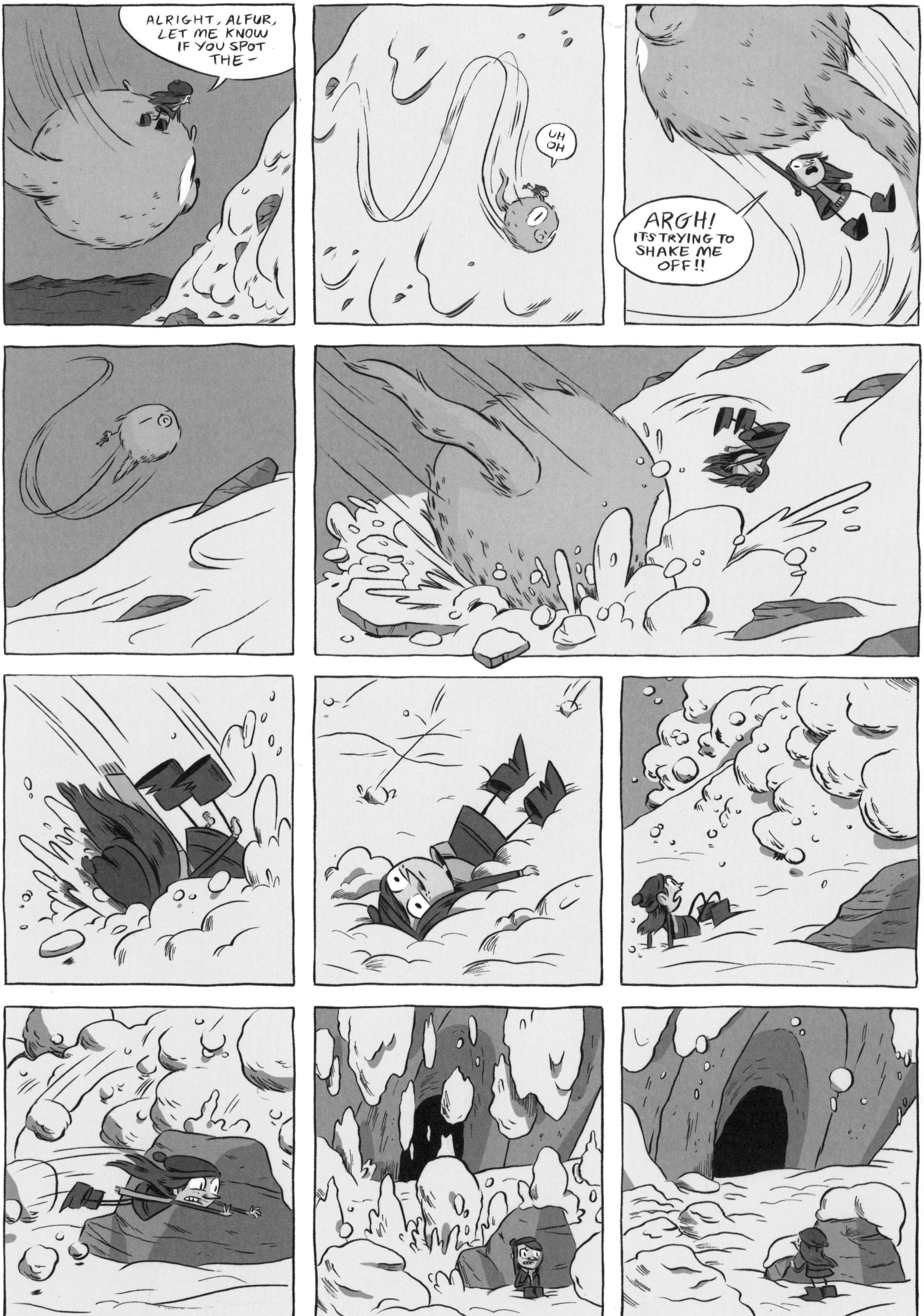
ALRIGHT, ALFUR, LET ME KNOW IF YOU SPOT THE -
UH OH
ARGH! ITS TRYING TO SHAKE ME OFF!!

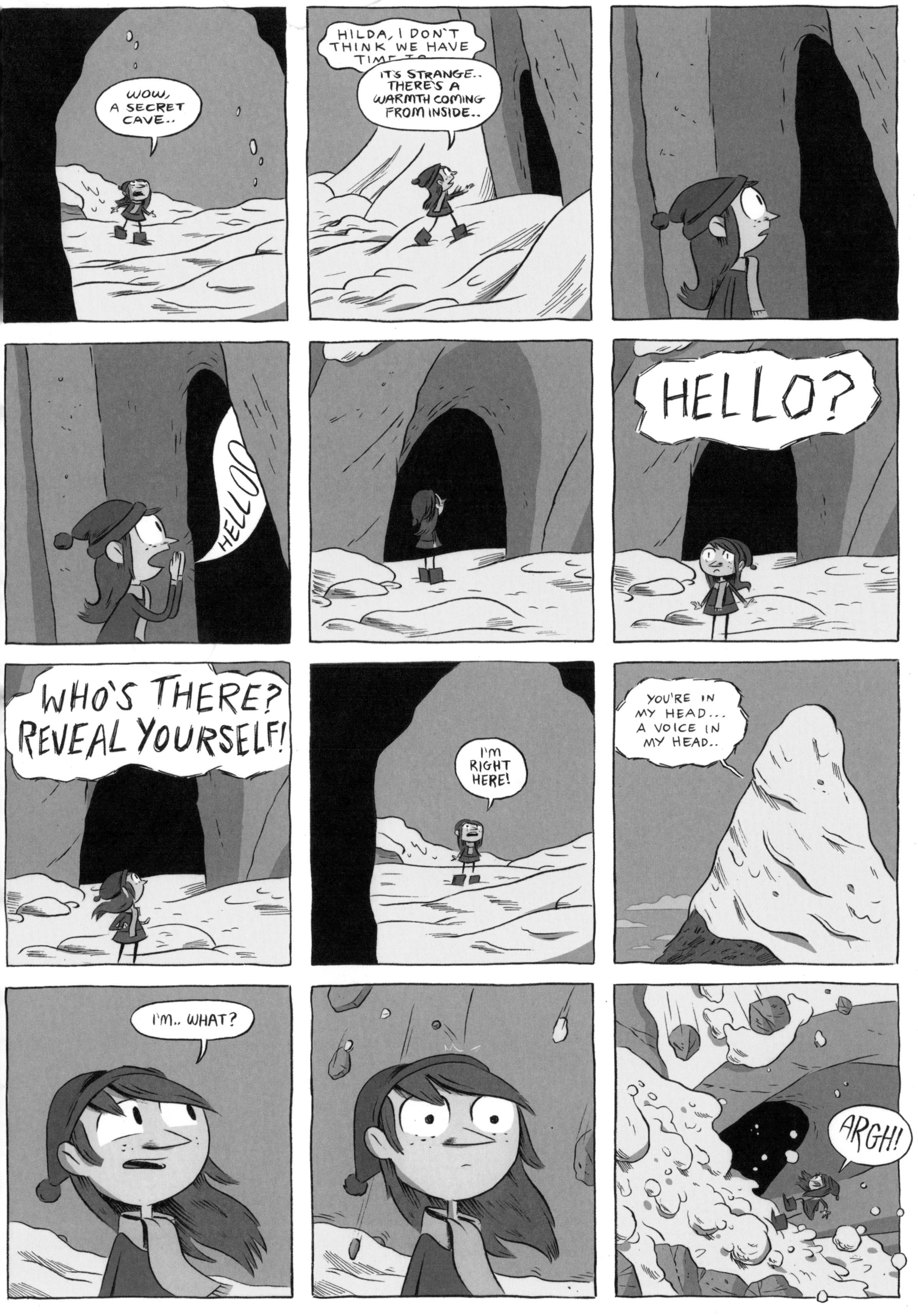
WOW, A SECRET CAVE..
HILDA, I DON'T THINK WE HAVE TIME TO
IT'S STRANGE.. THERE'S A WARMTH COMING FROM INSIDE..
HELLOO
HELLO?
WHO'S THERE? REVEAL YOURSELF!
I'M RIGHT HERE!
YOU'RE IN MY HEAD... A VOICE IN MY HEAD..
I'M.. WHAT?
ARGH!

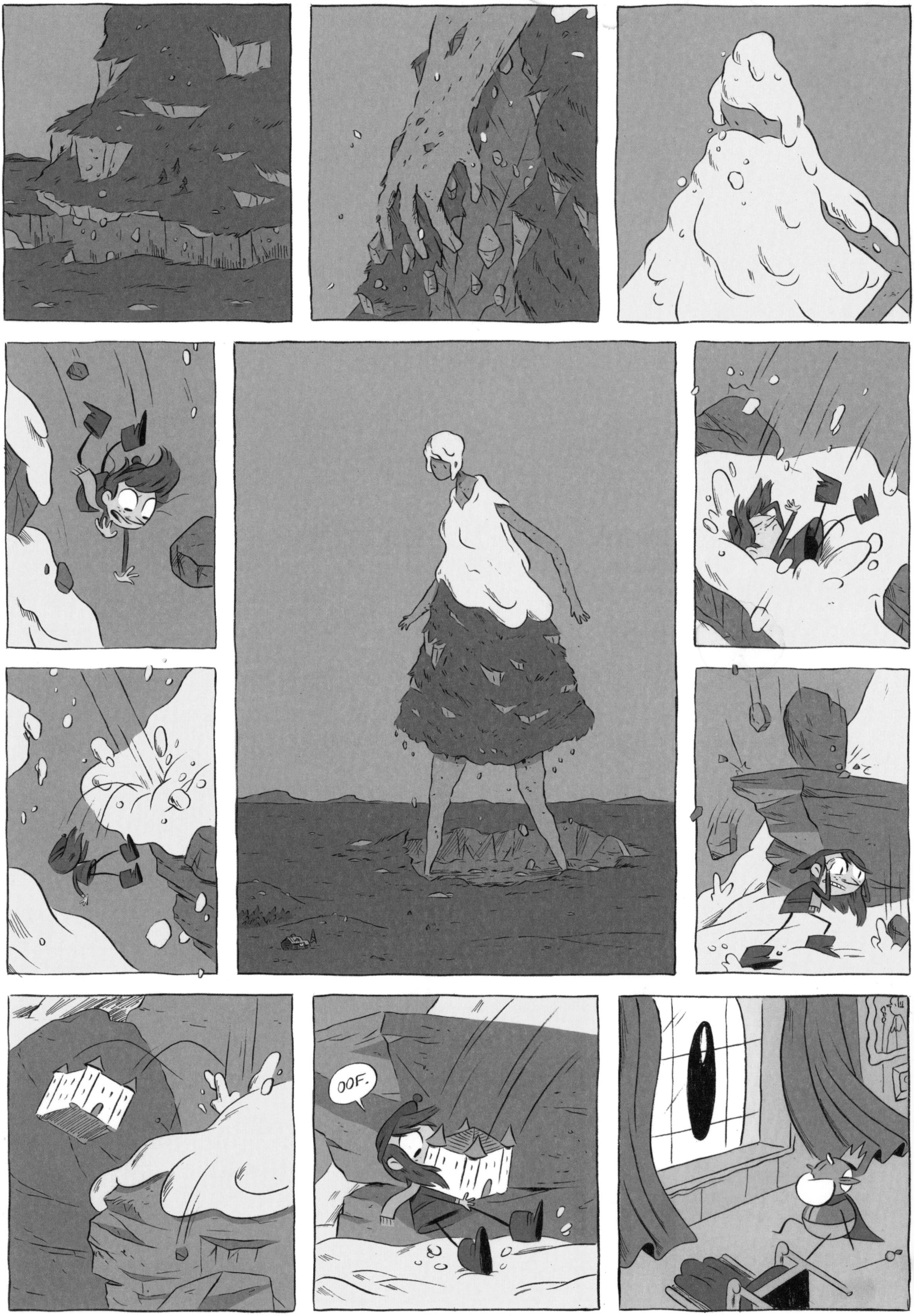
OOF.

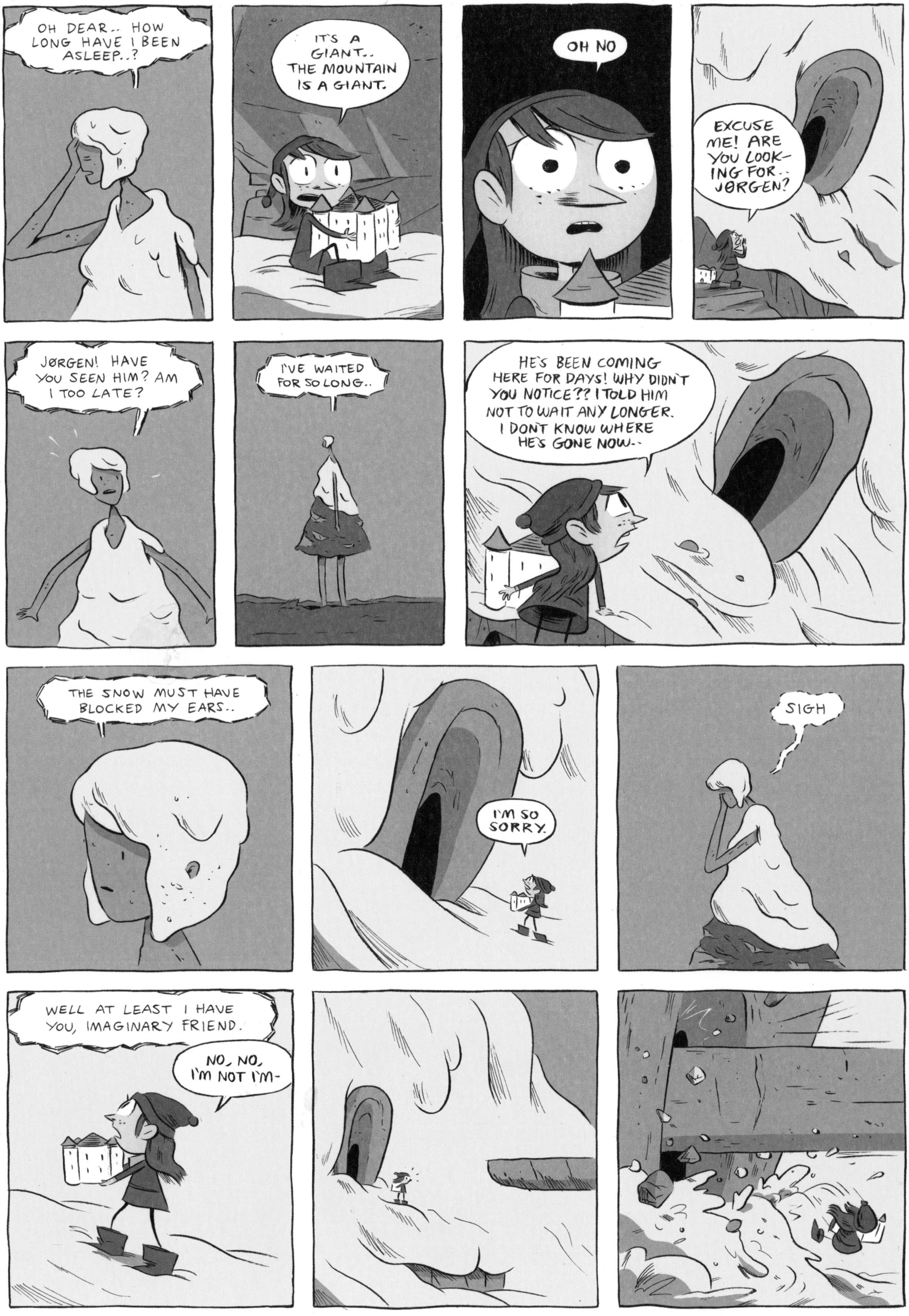

OH DEAR.. HOW LONG HAVE I BEEN ASLEEP..?
IT'S A GIANT.. THE MOUNTAIN IS A GIANT.
OH NO
EXCUSE ME! ARE YOU LOOKING FOR.. JØRGEN?
JØRGEN! HAVE YOU SEEN HIM? AM I TOO LATE?
I'VE WAITED FOR SO LONG..
HE'S BEEN COMING HERE FOR DAYS! WHY DIDN'T YOU NOTICE?? I TOLD HIM NOT TO WAIT ANY LONGER. I DON'T KNOW WHERE HE'S GONE NOW..
THE SNOW MUST HAVE BLOCKED MY EARS..
I'M SO SORRY.
SIGH
WELL AT LEAST I HAVE YOU, IMAGINARY FRIEND.
NO, NO, I'M NOT I'M-

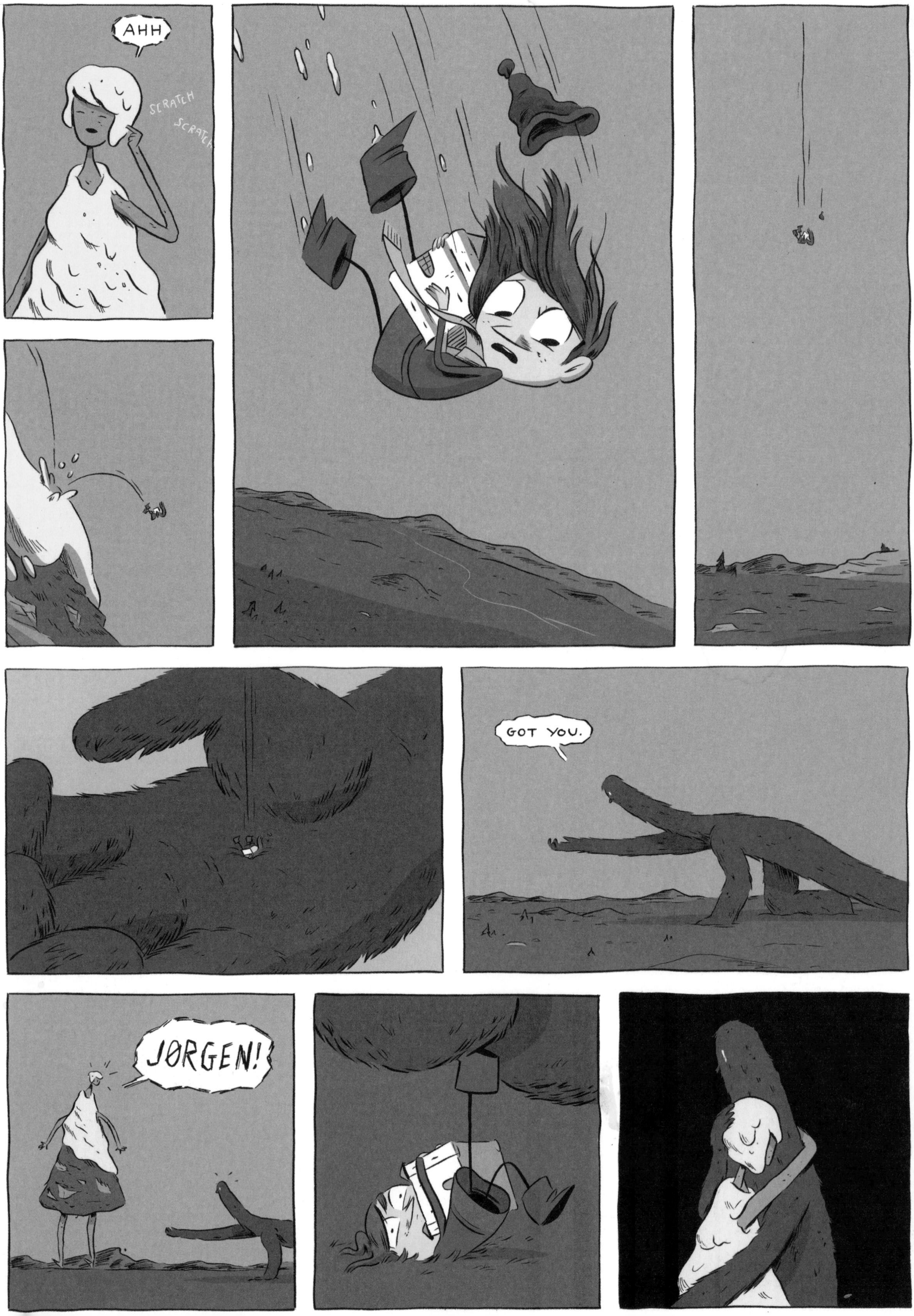
AHH
SCRATCH
SCRATCH
GOT YOU.
JØRGEN!

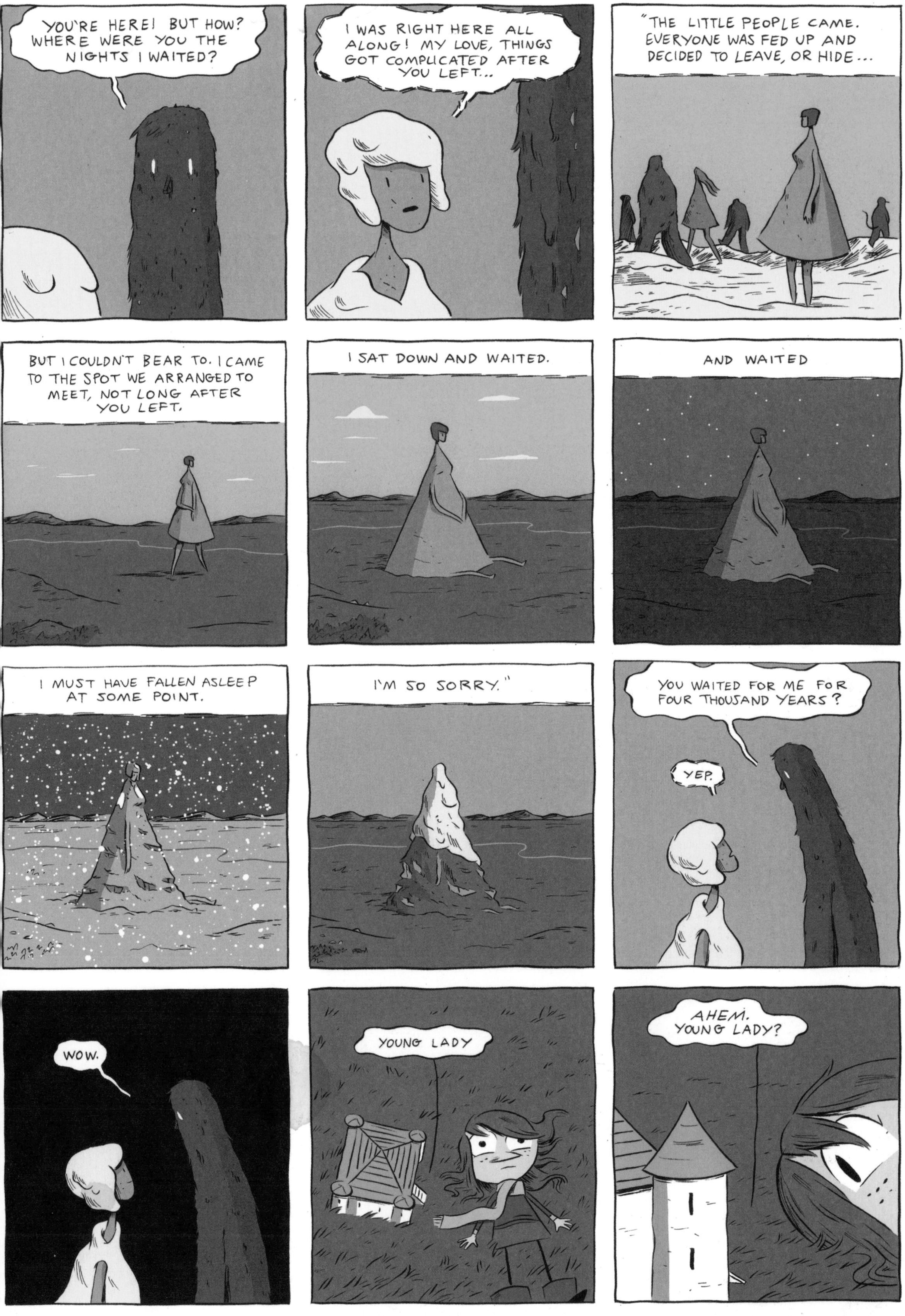
YOU'RE HERE! BUT HOW? WHERE WERE YOU THE NIGHTS I WAITED?
I WAS RIGHT HERE ALL ALONG! MY LOVE, THINGS GOT COMPLICATED AFTER YOU LEFT...
"THE LITTLE PEOPLE CAME. EVERYONE WAS FED UP AND DECIDED TO LEAVE, OR HIDE...
BUT I COULDN'T BEAR TO. I CAME TO THE SPOT WE ARRANGED TO MEET, NOT LONG AFTER YOU LEFT.
I SAT DOWN AND WAITED.
AND WAITED
I MUST HAVE FALLEN ASLEEP AT SOME POINT.
I'M SO SORRY."
YOU WAITED FOR ME FOR FOUR THOUSAND YEARS?
YEP.
WOW.
YOUNG LADY
AHEM. YOUNG LADY?

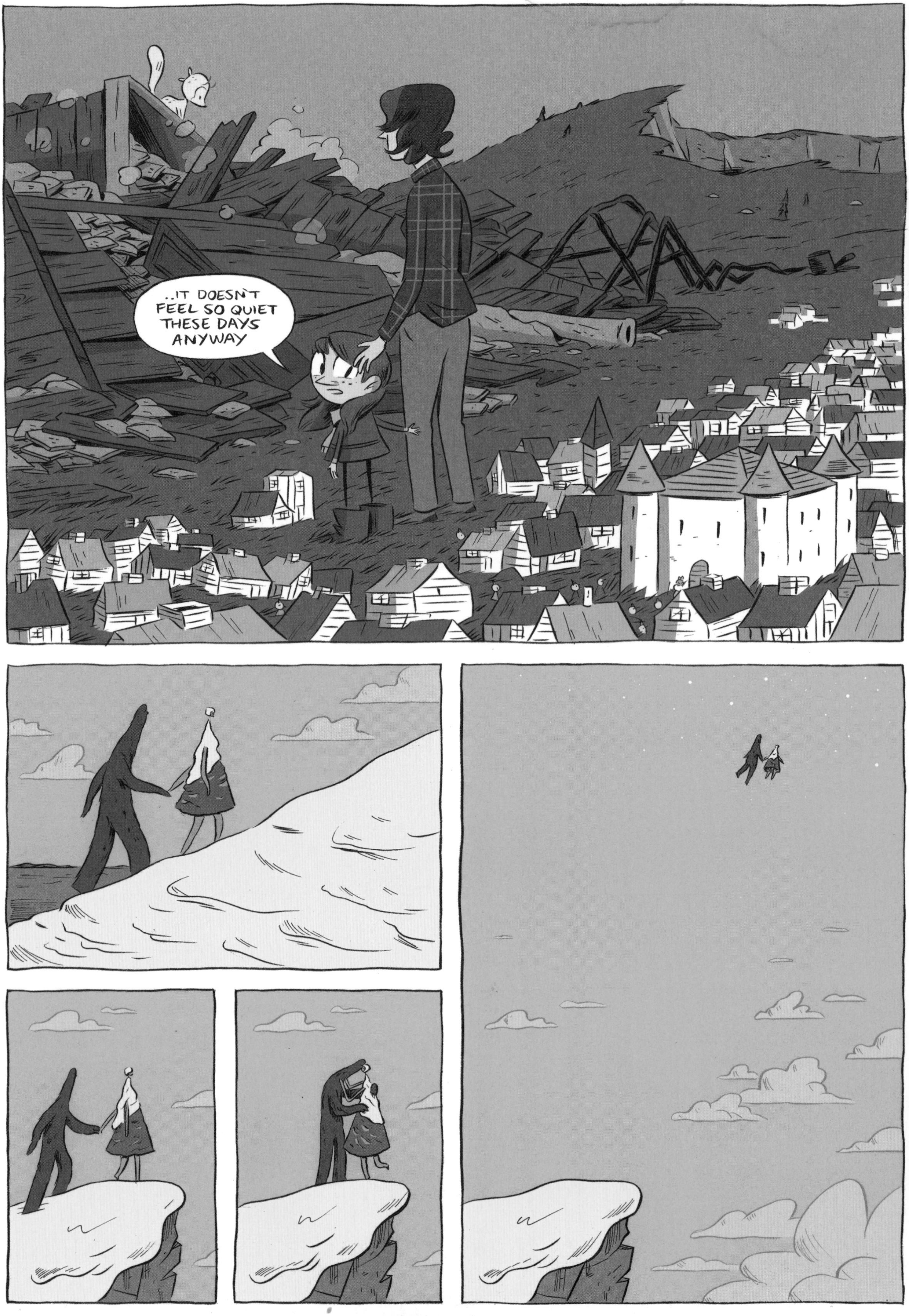
..IT DOESN'T FEEL SO QUIET THESE DAYS ANYWAY

FSC
www.fsc.org
MIX
Paper from responsible sources
FSC® C101807

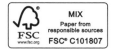

Thanks to Philippa, Alex, Sam, Judith, Isaac, everyone at Nobrow and my family.
Special thanks to Philippa Rice and Isaac Lenkiewicz for their help in colouring the book.

This is a sixth edition printed 2013.

Published by Flying Eye Books an imprint of Nobrow Ltd.
62 Great Eastern Street, London, EC2A 3QR

Printed in Belgium on FSC assured paper.

ISBN: 978-1-909263-17-8

Order from www.flyingeyebooks.com

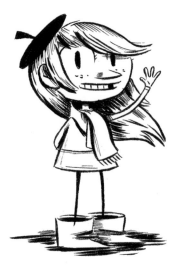

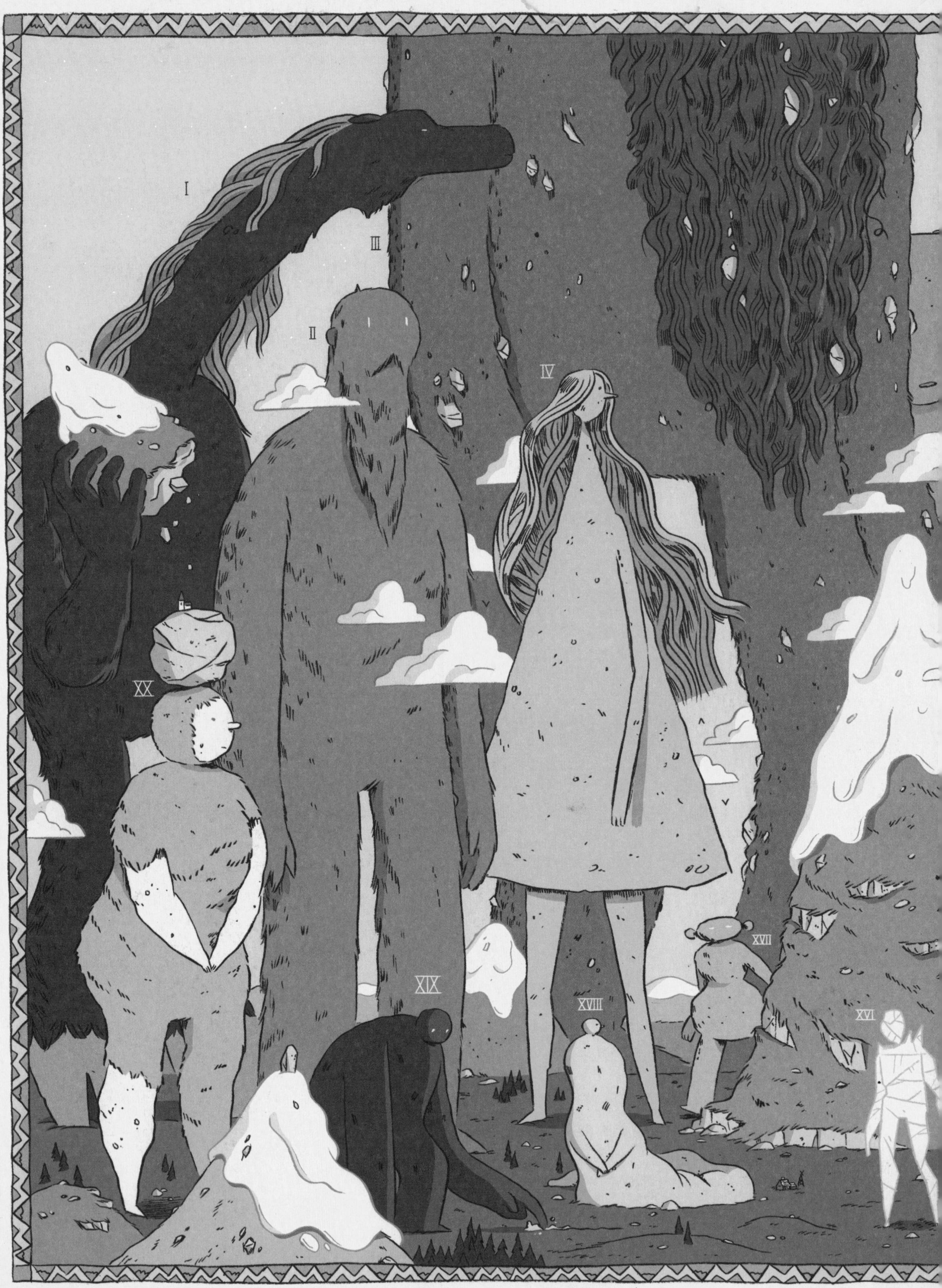

I
III
II
IV
XX
XIX
XVIII
XVII
XVI

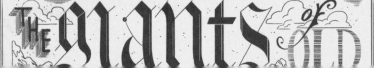

The Giants of Old

I **Fjällmarr** – Father of horses and dragons. Wilder and less forgiving than his fellow giants, he was a great anta of the little people, who feared him greatly. II **Aldinn** – Looked to by the other giants as a leader of sorts. He w first to take the leap and leave the valleys for good. III **Hár** – The oldest of the last generation of giants and by f largest. His ancient beard was home to a thriving, alien ecosystem. Many of the stranger creatures that wand Earth first appeared after they tumbled out of it. IV **Valfreyja** – Gardener and planter of trees. The first mou were sculpted in her appearance. V **Halldór** – Descended from a line of great warrior giants, he was actually the most gentle. He was greatly sympathetic to the little people and is the giant most fondly remembered in